"The Chronarchy

is a conscious experiment. Time and Matter are both ideas. Matter makes a more immediate impression on Man, but Time's effects are longer lasting. Therefore the Chronarchy, down the ages, has sought to educate its people into thinking of Time in a similar way as they think of Matter. In this way it has been possible to produce a science of time, like the science of physics. But it has only been possible to study time until now—not manipulate it.

"We may soon master Time as we once mastered the atom. And our mastery will give us far greater freedom than did our nuclear science. Time may be explored as our ancestors explored space. Your descendants shall be heir to continents of time as we have continents of space. They shall travel about in time, the old view of Past, Present and Future abolished . . .

"You are the first of the Time Dwellers and I salute you as the salvation of mankind."

MICHAEL MOORCOCK

THE
TIME
DWELLER

———————•═➤═•———————

Michael Moorcock

DAW BOOKS, INC.
DONALD A. WOLLHEIM, PUBLISHER
New York

ACKNOWLEDGMENTS: *The Time Dweller, Escape from Evening, The Golden Barge, Consuming Passion, The Ruins, The Pleasure Garden of Felipe Sagittarius,* and *The Mountain* © 1963, 1964, 1965, 1966 by New Worlds. *The Deep Fix* © 1963 by Science Fantasy. *Wolf* © 1966 by Compact Books.

FIRST DAW PRINTING, SEPTEMBER 1979

1 2 3 4 5 6 7 8 9

Contents

For Maeve, Claire, Sebastian and Fabian Peake and in love and admiation for Mervyn Peake, who died 17th November 1968, a generous man in an ungenerous world.

The Time Dweller

Dusk had come to the universe, albeit the small universe inhabited by Man. The sun of Earth had dimmed, the moon had retreated and salt clogged the sluggish oceans, filled the rivers that toiled slowly between white, crystalline banks, beneath darkened, moody skies that slumbered in eternal evening.

Of course, in the sun's long life this stage was merely one interlude. In perhaps a few thousand years, it would flare to full splendour again. But for the meantime it kept its light in close rein, grumbling in its mighty depths and preparing itself for the next step in its evolution.

It had taken time in its fading and those few creatures who had remained on its planets had managed to adapt. Among them was Man, indefatigable; undeserving, really, considering the lengths he had gone to in previous epochs, to dispose of himself. But here he was, in his small universe consisting of one planet without even the satellite which had slid away into space long since and, in its passing, left legends on his lips.

Brown clouds, brown light, brown rocks and brown ocean flecked with white. A pale rider on a pale beast thumping along the shore, the dry taste of ocean salt in his mouth, the stink of a dead oozer in his nostrils.

His name was the Scar-faced Brooder, son of the Sleepy-eyed Smiler, his father and the Pinch-cheeked Worrier, his mother. The seal-beast he rode was called Urge. Its glossy coat was still sleek with the salt-rain that had recently ceased, its snout pointed eagerly forward and its two strong leg-fins thwacked the encrusted shore as it galloped along, dragging its razor-edged tail with scant effort. The Scar-faced Brooder was supported on his steed's sloping back by a built-up saddle of polished silicon that flashed whenever it reflected the salt-

7

patches studding the ground like worn teeth. In his head, held at its butt by a stirrup grip, was his long gun, the piercer with an everlasting ruby as its life. He was dressed in sealskin dyed in sombre rust-red and dark yellow.

Behind him, the Scar-faced Brooder heard the sound of another rider, one whom he had tried to avoid since morning.

Now, as evening quietly flowed brown and misty into black night, she still followed. He turned his calm face to look, his mouth tight and white as the scar which rose from its corner to follow his left cheek-bone. She was in the distance, still, but gaining.

He increased his speed.

Brown clouds boiled low like foam across the dark sand of the flat, and their seals slapped loudly over the damp shore as she neared him.

He came to a pool of salt-thick water and Urge splashed into it. It was warm. Still she followed him, even into the water, so that he turned his steed and waited, half-trembling, until she rode up, a tall, well-formed woman with light brown hair long and loose in the breeze.

"Dearest Tall Laughter," he told his sister, "for me there is no amusement in this game."

Frowning, she smiled.

He pressed his point, disturbed, his calm face earnest in the fading brown light that was all the clouds would let pass.

"I wish to ride alone."

"Where would you go, alone, when together we might be carried to more exotic adventure?"

He paused, unwilling and unable to answer.

"Will you come back?"

"I would prefer not to."

A cold, silent wind began to buffet them as it came in suddenly from the sea. Urge moved nervously.

"You fear what the Chronarch might do?"

"The Chronarch has no love for me—but neither has he hatred. He would prefer me gone from Lanjis Liho, to cross the great salt plains of the west and seek my fortune in the land of fronds. He would not trust me with a small part of the Future, as you know, nor give a fraction of the Past into my safekeeping. I go to shape my own destiny!"

"So—you sulk!" she cried as the wind began to mewl.

"You sulk because the Chronarch delegates no honours. Meanwhile, your loving sister aches and is miserable."

"Marry the Big-brained Boaster! He has trust of Past and Future both!"

He forced his restless seal-beast through the thick water and into the night. As it moved, he reached into the saddle sheath and took out his torch to light his way. He depressed its grip and it blazed out, illuminating the surrounding beach for several yards around. Turning, he saw her for a moment in the circle of light, motionless, her eyes aghast as if he had betrayed her.

Oh, I am lonely now, he thought, as the wind blew cold and strong against his body.

He headed inland, over the salt-rocks, towards the west. He rode all night until his eyes were heavy with tiredness, but still he rode, away from Lanjis Liho where Chronarch, Lord of Time, ruled past and present and watched the future come, away from family, home and city, his heart racked with the strain of the breaking, his mind fevered fire and his body all stiff from the demands he made of it.

Into the night, into the west, with his torch burning in his saddle and loyal Urge responding to his affectionate whispering. To the west, until dawn came slowly up from behind him and covered the barren land with soft light.

A little further through the morning he heard a sound as of cloth flapping in the wind and when he turned his head he saw a green tent pitched beside a shallow crevasse, its front flap dancing. He readied his long piercer and halted Urge.

Drawn out, perhaps, by the noise of the seal-beast's movement, a man's head poked from the tent like a tortoise emerging from the recesses of its shell. He had a beak of a nose and a fish-like pecker of a mouth, his large eyes were heavy-lidded and a tight-fitting hood hid hair and neck.

"Aha," said the Scar-faced Brooder in recognition.

"Hmm," said the Hooknosed Wanderer, also recognizing the mounted man confronting him. "You are some distance from Lanjis Liho. Where are you bound?"

"For the land of fronds."

He resheathed his piercer and clambered down from the high saddle. He passed the tent, its occupant's head craning round to follow him and stared into the crevasse. It had been widened and deepened by human tools, revealing pieces of ancient wreckage. "What's this?"

"Nothing but the remains of a crashed spaceship," replied the Hooknosed Wanderer in such obvious disappointment that he could not have been lying. "My metal diviner found it and I had hoped for a capsule with books or film."

"There were never many of those. I'd say they had all been gathered by now."

"That's my belief, too, but one hopes. Have you breakfasted?"

"No. Thank you."

The hooded head withdrew into the tent and a thin hand held back the flap. The Scar-faced Brooder bent and entered the cluttered tent. There was a great deal of equipment therein; the Hooknosed Wanderer's livelihood, for he sustained himself by bartering some of the objects he found with his metal diviner and other instruments.

"Apparently, you have no riding animal," said the Scar-faced Brooder as he sat down and crossed his legs between a soft bundle and an angular statuette of steel and concrete.

"It was necessary to abandon her when my water was exhausted and I could find none to replace it. That is why I was heading for the sea. I am exceedingly thirsty, am suffering from salt-deficiency since I have no liking for the salt which grows in these parts."

"I have plenty in my saddle barrel," he said. "Help yourself—good salt water, slightly diluted with fresh, if that suits your taste." He leant back on the bundle as the Wanderer, nodding sharply, scrambled up, clasping a canteen and left the tent.

He returned smiling. "Thanks. I can last for several days, now." He pushed aside his clutter of antiques, discovering a small stove. He activated it, placed a pan on top and began frying the leg-fish he had trapped recently.

"Which city was your destination, Brooder? Only two are in easy reach from here—and both lie still many leagues hence. Is it Barbart or Piorha?"

"Barbart in the land of fronds, I think, for I should like to see green vegetation instead of grey or brown. And the ancient places thereabouts have, I must admit, romantic connotations for me. I should like to go and wallow in racial memory, sense the danger of uncontrolled Past, insignificant Present and random Future . . ."

"Some feel it as that," the Wanderer smiled, shuffling the leg-fish on to plates. "Especially those from Lanjis Liho where the Chronarchy holds sway. But remember, much will be in your mind. You may see Barbart and the land of fronds, but its significance will be decided by you, not by it. Try to do as I do—make no judgments or descriptions of this world of ours. Do that, and it will treat you better."

"Your words seem wise, Wanderer, but I have no precedents by which to judge them. Perhaps when I have placed some of the Future in the Past, I will know."

"You seem tired," said the Wanderer when they finished eating, "would you like to sleep?"

"I would. Thanks." And while the Hooknosed Wanderer went about his business, the Brooder slept.

He rose in the mellow afternoon, roused Urge who had taken advantage of his master's slumber to rest also, and wished the Wanderer goodbye.

"May your blood stay thick," said the Wanderer formally, "and your mind remain open."

He rode a way and by dusk had come to the moss which was primarily grey and brown, but tinted in places with patches of light green. He took out his torch and fixed it in its saddle bracket, unwilling to sleep at night because of the potential danger of predatory life.

Once the light from his torch showed him a school of oozers, moving at right angles to his path. They were far inland for their kind, these great white slug-creatures that raised their heads to observe him. He felt he could hear them sniffing at his body salt as perhaps their leech ancestors had sniffed out the blood of his own forefathers. Urge, without prompting, increased his speed.

As he left them, he felt that the oozers represented the true native of Earth now. Man's place was no longer easy to define, but it seemed that he had been superseded. By remaining alive on the salt-heavy Earth he was outstaying his welcome. If there was another home for Man, it did not lie here but in some other region; perhaps not even the region of space at all but in dimensions where natural evolution could not affect him.

Brooding, as was his bent, he continued to ride for Barbart

and, by the following day, had reached the delicate frond
forests that waved golden green in the soft sunlight, all
silence and sweet scent. Urge's bounding gait became almost
merry as they fled over the cushions of moss between the
shaded spaces left by the web-thin fronds waving and flowing
in the gusts of air which occasionally swept the forest.

He dismounted soon and lay back on a bank of comfortable moss, breathing the scented breeze in luxurious self-in-
dulgence. His mind began to receive disjointed images, he
heard his sister's voice, the sonorous tones of the Chronarch
denying him a function in the House of Time—a function
which he had expected as of right, for had not his grand-
uncle been the previous Chronarch? He saw the twisting
many dimensioned Tower of Time, that wonder-work of an
ancient architect with its colours and strange, moving angles
and curves. And then he slept.

When he awoke it was night and Urge was hooting at him to
wake. He got up sleepily and hauled himself into the saddle,
settled himself, reached for his torch and adjusting it rode
through what seemed to be a network of black and stirring
threads that were the fronds seen in the cold torch-light.

The next morning he could see the low-roofed houses of
Barbart lying in a valley walled by gentle hills. High above
the roofs, a great contrivance of burnished brass glowered
like rich red gold. He speculated momentarily upon its function.

Now a road became evident, a hard track winding among
the moss dunes and leading towards the city. As he followed
it he heard the muffled thud of a rider approaching and,
somewhat wary for he knew little of Barbart or its inhabitants, reined in Urge, his piercer ready.

Riding towards him on a heavy old walrus came a young
man, long-haired and pleasant-featured in a jerkin of light
blue that matched his eyes. He stopped the walrus and looked
quizzically at the Scar-faced Brooder.

"Stranger," he said cheerfully, "it is a pleasant morning."

"Yes, it is—and a pleasant land you dwell in. Is that city
Barbart?"

"Barbart, certainly. There's none other hereabouts. From
where are you?"

"From Lanjis Liho by the sea."

"I had the inkling that men from Lanjis Liho never travelled far."

"I am the first. My name is the Scar-faced Brooder."

"Mine is Domm and I welcome you to Barbart. I would escort you there save for the fact that I have a mission from my mother to seek herbs among the fronds. I am already late, I fear. What time is it?"

"Time? Why the present, of course."

"Ha! Ha! But the hour—what is that?"

"What is 'the hour'?" asked the Brooder, greatly puzzled.

"That's my question."

"I am afraid your local vernacular is beyond me," said the Brooder politely, but nonplussed. The lad's question had been strange to begin with, but now it had become incomprehensible.

"No matter," Domm decided with a smile. "I have heard you people of Lanjis Liho have some peculiar customs. I will not delay you. Follow the road and you should be in Barbart in less than an hour."

"Hour"—the word again. Was it some division of the league used here? He gave up wondering and wished the youth "thick blood" as he rode on.

The mosaiced buildings of Barbart were built in orderly geometric patterns about the central quadrangle in which lay the towering machine of burnished brass with its ridges and knobs and curlicues. Set in the centre of the machine was a great round plaque, divided into twelve units with each unit of twelve divided into a further five units. From the centre arose two points, one shorter than the other and the Scar-faced Brooder saw them move slowly. As he rode through Barbart, he noticed that facsimiles of this object were everywhere and he judged, at last, that it was some holy object or heraldic device.

Barbart seemed a pleasant place, though with a somewhat restless atmosphere epitomized by the frantic market-place where men and women rushed from stall to stall shouting at one another, tugging at bales of bright cloth, fingering salt-free fruits and vegetables, pawing meats and confectionaries amid the constant babble of the vendors crying their wares.

Enjoying the scene, the Scar-faced Brooder led his sealbeast through the square and discovered a tavern in one of the side plazas. The plaza itself contained a small fountain in its centre and benches and tables had been placed close by outside the tavern. The Brooder seated himself upon one of these and gave his order to the fat girl who came to ask it.

"Beer?" she said, folding her plump, brown arms over her red bodice. "We have only a little and it is expensive. The fermented peach juice is cheaper."

"Then bring me that," he said pleasantly and turned to watch the thin fountain water, noting that it smelt of brine hardly at all.

Hearing, perhaps, a strange accent, a man emerged from the shadowy doorway of the tavern and, tankard in hand, stood looking down at the Scar-faced Brooder, an amiable expression on his face.

"Where are you from, traveller?" he asked.

The Brooder told him and the Barbartian seemed surprised. He seated himself on another bench.

"You are the second visitor from strange parts we have had here in a week. The other was an emissary from Moon. They have changed much, those Moonites, you know. Tall, they are, and thin as a frond with aesthetic faces. They dress in cloth of metal. He told us he had sailed space for many weeks to reach us . . ."

At this second reference to the unfamiliar word "week", the Brooder turned his head to look at the Barbartian. "Forgive me," he said, "but as a stranger I am curious at certain words I have heard here. What would you mean by 'week' exactly?"

"Why—a week—seven days—what else?"

The Brooder laughed apologetically. "There you are, you see. Another word—days. What is a days?"

The Barbartian scratched his head, a wry expression on his face. He was a middle-aged man with a slight stoop, dressed in a robe of yellow cloth. He put down his tankard and raised his hand. "Come with me and I will do my best to show you."

"That would please me greatly," said the Brooder gratefully. He finished his wine and called for the girl. When she appeared he asked her to take care of his steed and to make him up a bed since he would be staying through the next darkness.

The Barbartian introduced himself as Mokof, took the Brooder's arm and led him through the series of squares, and triangles and circles formed by the buildings, to come at length to the great central plaza and stare up at the pulsing, monstrous machine of burnished bronze.

"This machine supplies the city with its life," Mokof informed him. "And also regulates our lives." He pointed at the disc which the Brooder had noted earlier. "Do you know what this is, my friend?"

"No, I am afraid I do not. Could you explain?"

"It's a *clock*. It measures the hours of the day," he broke off, noting the Brooder's puzzlement. "That is to say it measures time."

"Ah! I am with you at last. But a strange device, surely, for it cannot measure a great deal of time with that little circular dial. How does it note the flow . . .?"

"We call a period of sunlight 'day' and a period of darkness 'night.' We divide each into twelve hours—"

"Then the period of sunlight and the period of darkness are equal? I had thought . . ."

"No, we call them equal for convenience, since they vary. The twelve divisions are called hours. When the hands reach twelve, they begin to count around again . . ."

"Fantastic!" the Brooder was astounded. "You mean you recycle the same period of time round and round again. A marvellous idea. Wonderful! I had not thought it possible."

"Not exactly," Mokof said patiently. "However, the hours are divided into sixty units. These are called minutes. The minutes are also divided into sixty units, each unit is called a second. The seconds are . . ."

"Stop! Stop! I am confounded, bewildered, dazzled! How do you control the flow of time that you can thus manipulate it at will? You must tell me. The Chronarch in Lanjis Liho would be overawed to learn of your discoveries!"

"You fail to understand, my friend. We do not *control* time. If anything, it controls us. We simply measure it."

"You don't control . . . but if that's so why—?" The Brooder broke off, unable to see the logic of the Barbartian's words. "You tell me you recycle a given period of time which you divided into twelve. And yet you then tell me you recycle a shorter period and then an even shorter period. It would soon become apparent if this were true, for you would be performing the same action over and over again and I see you are not. Or, if you were using the same time without being in its power, the sun would cease to move across the sky and I see it still moves. Given that you can release yourself from the influence of time, why am I not conscious of it since that instrument," he pointed at the *clock*, "exerts its influence over the entire city. Or, again, if it is a natural talent, why are we in Lanjis Liho so busily concerned with categorizing and investigating our researches into the flow if you have mastered it so completely?"

A broad smile crossed the face of Mokof. He shook his head. "I told you—we have no mastery over it. The instrument merely tells us what time it is."

"That is ridiculous," the Brooder said, dazed. His brain fought to retain its sanity. "There is only the present. Your words are illogical!"

Mokof stared at his face in concern. "Are you unwell?"

"I'm well enough. Thank you for the trouble you have taken, I will return to the tavern now, before I lose all hold of sanity!"

The clutter in his head was too much. Mokof made a statement and then denied it in the same breath. He decided he would cogitate it over a meal.

When he reached the tavern he found the door closed and no amount of banging could get those inside to open it. He noticed that his saddle and saddle-bags were resting outside and he knew he had some food in one of the bags, so he sat on the bench and began to munch on a large hunk of bread.

Suddenly, from above him, he heard a cry and looking up he saw an old woman's head regarding him from a top-storey window.

"Ah!" she cried. "Aah! What are you doing?"

"Why, eating this piece of bread, madame," he said in surprise.

"Filthy!" she shrieked. "Filthy, immoral pig!"

"Really, I fail to—"

"Watch! Watch!" the old woman cried from the window.

Very swiftly, three armed men came running into the plaza. They screwed up their faces in disgust when they saw the Scar-faced Brooder.

"A disgusting exhibitionist as well as a pervert!" said the leader.

They seized the startled Brooder.

"What's happening?" he gasped. "What have I done?"

"Ask the judge," snarled one of his captors and they

hauled him towards the cental plaza and took him to a tall
house which appeared to be their headquarters.

There he was flung into a cell and they went away.

An overdressed youth in the next cell said with a grin:
"Greetings, stranger. What's your offence?"

"I have no idea," said the Brooder. "I merely sat down to
have my lunch when, all at once . . ."

"Your lunch? But it is not lunch-time for another ten
minutes!"

"Lunch-time. You mean you set aside a special period to
eat—oh, this is too much for me."

The overdressed youth drew away from the bars and went
to the other side of his cell, his nose wrinkling in disgust.
"Ugh—you deserve the maximum penalty for a crime like
that!"

Sadly puzzled, the Brooder sat down on his bench, completely mystified and hopeless. Evidently the strange customs
of these people were connected with their *clock* which
seemed to be a virtual deity to them. If the hands did not
point to a certain figure when you did something, then that
act became an offence. He wondered what the maximum
penalty would be.

Very much later, the guards came to him and made him walk
through a series of corridors and into a room where a man in
a long purple gown wearing a metallic mask was seated at a
carved table. The guards made the Brooder sit before the
man and then they went and stood by the door.

The masked man said in a sonorous voice: "You have
been accused of eating outside the proper hour and of doing
it in a public place for all to see. A serious charge. What is
your defence?"

"Only that I am a stranger and do not understand your
customs," said the Brooder.

"A poor excuse. Where are you from?"

"From Lanjis Liho by the sea."

"I have heard rumours of the immoralities practised there.
You will learn that you cannot bring your filthy habits to another city and hope to continue with them. I will be lenient
with you, however, and sentence you to one year in the an-
tique mines."

"But it is unjust!"

"Unjust, is it? Watch your tongue or I will extend the sentence!"

Depressed and without hope, the Brooder allowed the guards to take him back to his cell.

The night passed and morning came and then the guards arrived. "Get up," said the leader, "the judge wishes to see you again!"

"Does he intend to increase my sentence, after all?"

"Ask him."

The judge was tapping his desk nervously as the Brooder and his guards entered.

"You know of machines in Lanjis Liho, do you not? You have some strange ones I've heard. Do you wish to be released?"

"I wish to be released, of course. Yes, we know something of machines, but . . ."

"Our Great Regulator is out of control. I would not be surprised if your crime did not provide the shock which caused it to behave erratically. Something has gone wrong with its life core and we may have to evacuate Barbart if it cannot be adjusted. We have forgotten our old knowledge of machines. If you adjust the Great Regulator, we shall let you go. Without it, we do not know when to sleep, eat or perform any of our other functions. We shall go mad if we lose its guidance!"

Scarcely understanding the rest of the judge's statement, the Brooder heard only the fact that he was to be released if he mended their machine. On the other hand, he had left Lanjis Liho for the very reason that the Chronarch would not give him trust of any instruments. He had little experience yet, if it meant his relaese, he would try.

When he arrived again in the central plaza, he noted that the machine of burnished bronze—the Great Regulator, they called it—was making a peculiar grumbling noise and shaking mightily. Around it, trembling in unison, stood a dozen old men, waving their hands.

"Here is the man from Lanjis Liho!" called the guard. They looked anxiously at the Scar-faced Brooder.

"The life-core. It must certainly be the life-core," said an ancient, tugging at his jerkin.

"Let me see," said the Scar-faced Brooder, not at all sure that he could be of help.

They wound off several of the machine's outer plates and he stared through thick glass and looked at the luminous life-core. He had seen them before and knew a little about them. He knew enough, certainly, to understand that this should not be glowing bright purple and showering particles with such constancy.

He knew, suddenly, that in an exceedingly short space of time—one of these people's 'minutes', perhaps—the life-core would reach a critical state, it would swell and burst from its confines and its radiation would destroy everything living. But, he ignored their shouts as he became lost in the problem; he would need considerably longer than that if he was to deal with it.

Soon, he realized helplessly, they would all be dead.

He turned to tell them this, and then it struck him. Why could not he, as he had guessed these citizens capable of, *recycle* that moment, personally?

Since the previous day, his mind had been trying to see the logic in what Mokof had told him and, using parts of things the Chronarch had told him, he had constructed an idea of what the process must be like.

Experimentally, he eased himself *backwards* in time. Yes, it worked. The core was now as he had first seen it.

He had never thought of doing this before, but now he saw that it was easy, requiring merely a degree of concentration. He was grateful for the Barbartians, with their weird time device, for giving him the idea.

All he had to do was to remember what the Chronarch had taught him about the nature of time—how it constantly and imperceptibly to ordinary beings re-formed its constituents to give it the apparently forward movement which affected, so broadly, the organization of matter.

Shifting himself into the time-area he had occupied a short while before, he began to study the temporal co-ordinates of the life-core. He could think of no physical means of stopping it, but if he could in some manner lock it in time, it would then cease to be a danger. But he would still have to work speedily, since, sooner or later, the temporal structure would fail to hold and he would sweep onwards, losing time continuously, until he was brought to the moment when the life-core began to spread its radiation.

Again and again he let himself drift up almost to the ultimate moment, shifting himself backwards, losing a few grains of time with every shift.

Then, at last, he understood the temporal construction of the core. With an effort of will he reduced the temporal coordinates to zero. It could not progress through time. It was frozen and no longer a danger.

He fell back into his normal time-stream, his body wet with sweat. They crowded about him, questioning in shrill, excited voices.

"What have you done? What have you done? Are we safe?"

"You are safe," he said.

They seized him, thanking him with generous words, his earlier crime forgotten. "You must be rewarded."

But he scarcely heard them, as they bore him back to the judge, for he was brooding on what he had just accomplished.

As a man might step backwards to regain lost ground, he had stepped backwards to regain lost time. He had his reward. He was most grateful to these people now, for with their weird ideas about time, they had shown him that it was possible to exist at will in a point in time—just as it was possible to exist in a point in space. It was, he realized merely a matter of *knowing* such a thing was possible. Then it became easy.

The judge had doffed his mask and smiled his gratitude. "The wise men tell me that you worked a miracle. They saw your body flickering like a candle flame, disappearing and appearing constantly. How did you achieve this?"

He spread his hands: "It was extraordinarily simple. Until I came to Barbart and saw the thing you call *clock*, I did not realize the possibilities of moving through time as I could move through space. It seemed to me that since you appeared capable of recycling the same period of time, I could do likewise. This I did. Then I studied the life-core and saw that, by manipulation of its time structure, I could fix it in a certain point, thus arresting its progress. So simple—and yet it might never have occurred to me if I had not come here."

The judge passed a hand over his puzzled eyes. "Ah . . ." he said.

"And now," the Brooder said cheerfuly, "I thank you for your hospitality. I intend to leave Barbart immediately, since I shall obviously never understand your customs. I return to Lanjis Liho to tell the Chronarch of my discoveries. Farewell."

He left the court-room, crossed the plaza through crowds of grateful citizens, and was soon saddling Urge and riding away from Barbart in the land of fronds.

Two days later he came upon the Hooknosed Wanderer grubbing in a ditch he had just dug.

"Greetings, Wanderer," he called from the saddle.

The Wanderer looked up, wiping salty earth from his face. "Oh, 'tis you, Brooder. I thought you had decided to journey to the land of fronds."

"I did. I went to Barbart and there—" briefly the Brooder explained what had happened.

"Aha," nodded the Wanderer. "So the Chronarch is educating his people well, after all. I frankly considered what he was doing impossible. But you have proved me wrong."

"What do you mean?"

"I think I can tell you. Come into my tent and drink some wine."

"Willingly," the Brooder said, dismounting.

From a plastic flask, the Wanderer poured wine into two cut-glass goblets.

"Lanjis Liho," he said, "was founded in ancient times as an experimental village where new-born children were taken and educated according to the teachings of a certain philosopher called Rashin. Rashin regarded people's attitude towards Time as being imposed on their consciousness by their method of recording and measuring it—by the state of mind which said 'the past is the past and cannot be changed,' 'we cannot know what the future holds' and so forth. Our minds, he decided, were biased and while we continued to think in this way we should never be free of the shackles of time. It was, he felt, the most necessary shackle to cast off. He said, for instance, that when the temperature becomes too hot, a man devises a means of keeping himself cool. When it rains he enters a shelter or devises a shelter he can transport with him. If he comes to a river, he builds a bridge, or if to the sea—a boat. Physical difficulties of a certain intensity can be overcome in a physical way. But what if the difficulties intensify to the degree where physical means can no longer work against them?"

The Brooder shrugged. "We perish—or find some means other than physical to combat them."

'Exactly. Rashin said that if Time moves too swiftly for a man to accomplish what he desires he accepts the fact passively. Rashin thought that with re-education Man might rid himself of his reconception and take as easily to adjusting Time to his requirements as he adjusts nature. A non-physical means you see."

"I think I understand a little of what you mean," said the Scar-faced Brooder. "But why is it necessary, I wonder?" The question was rhetorical, but the Wanderer chose to answer.

"On this world." he said, "we must admit it, Man is an anachronism. He has adapted to a degree but not sufficiently to the point where he could sustain himself without artifice. The planet has never been particularly suitable for him, of course, but it has never been so inhospitable as now.

"The Chronarchy, as I have said, is a conscious experiment. Time and Matter are both ideas. Matter makes a more immediate impression on Man, but Time's effects are longer lasting. Therefore the Chronarchy, down the ages, has sought to educate its people into thinking of Time in a similar way as they think of Matter. In this way it has been possible to produce a science of time, like the science of physics. But it has only been possible to study time until now—not manipulate it.

"We may soon master Time as we once mastered the atom. And our mastery will give us far greater freedom than did our nuclear science. Time may be explored as our ancestors explored space. Your descendants, Scar-faced Brooder, shall be heir to continents of time as we have continents of space. They shall travel about in time, the old view of Past, Present and Future abolished. Even now you regard these in an entirely different light—merely as convenient classifications for the study of Time."

"That is true," he nodded, "I had never considered them anything else. But now I am unsure what to do, for I fled to Barbart originally to settle and forget Lanjis Liho where I went unhonoured."

The Wanderer smiled a little. "I do not think you will go unhonoured now, my friend," he said.

The Brooder saw the point and smiled also. "Perhaps not," he agreed.

The Wandered sipped his wine. "Your journeyings in space are all but ended, anyway. For space is becoming increasingly hostile to Man and will soon refuse to sustain him, however much he adapts physically. You and your like must enter the new dimensions you've discovered and dwell there. Go back to Lanjis Liho of your birth and tell the Chronarch what you did in Barbart, *show* him what you did and he will welcome you. Your reason for leaving no longer exists. You are the first of the Time Dwellers and I salute you as the salvation of mankind." The Wanderer drained his glass.

Somewhat overwhelmed by this speech, the Brooder bade the Wanderer farewell and thick blood, left the tent and climbed upon the back of Urge.

The Wanderer stood beside the tent, smiling at him. "One day you must tell me how you did it," he said.

"It is such a simple thing—you just live through the same period of time instead of different ones. Perhaps this is just the start and soon I will be able to explore further abroad—or is the word 'a-time'? But now I will be off for I'm impatient to tell my news to the Chronarch!"

The Wanderer watched him ride away, feeling a trifle like the last dinosaur must have felt so many millions of years before.

Once again, the Scar-faced Brooder rode along the seashore, staring over the sluggish waves at the brown sky beyond.

Salt shone everywhere across the land, perhaps heralding an age where crystalline life-forms would develop in conditions absolutely unsuitable for animal life as he knew it.

Yes, the period when Man must change his environment radically had come, if Man were to survive at all.

The Earth would cease to support him soon, the sun cease to warm him. He had the choice of living for a while in artificial conditions such as the Moonites already did, or of completely changing his environment—from a physical one to a temporal one!

Definitely, the latter was the better choice. As the sky darkened over the sea, he took out his torch, depressed the handle and sent a great blaze of light spreading across the inhospitable Earth.

The first of the Time Dwellers goaded his seal-beast into a faster pace, impatient to tell the Chronarch his welcome news, impatient to begin the exploration of a new environment.

Escape From Evening

On Moon it was white like ice. An endless series of blocks
and spikes, like an ancient cubist painting. But white; glaring,
though the sun was almost dead, a red featureless disc in the
dark sky.

In his artificial cavern, full of synthetic, meaningless things
that contained no mythology or mood, Pepin Hunchback
bent over his book so that the tears from his eyes fell upon
the plastic pages and lay there glistening.

Of all the things that the glass cavern contained—pumps
and pipes and flinching dials—only Pepin had warmth. His
twisted body was a-throb with life and large emotions. His
imagination was alive and active as each word in the book
sparked off great chords of yearning within him. His narrow
face, utterly pale save for the bright black eyes, was intense.
His clumsy hands moved to turn the pages. He was dressed,
as were all his fellow Moonites, in cloth-of-metal which, with
a helmet fitted to its hauberk, protected his life from an impossibility—the threat of the System collapsing.

The System was Moon's imitation of life. It aped an older
Earth than that which now existed far away, barely visible in
space. It aped its plants and its animals and its elements—for
the System was Moon's artificial ecology. Moon was a planet
of goodish size—had been for centuries since it had ceased to
be Earth's satellite and had drifted into the asteroids and attracted many of them to itself.

And Pepin hated the System for what it was. Pepin was a
throw-back, unsuited to his present Time or Space. Pepin's
life was not the System, for with just that he would have
died. It was his imagination, his sorrow and his ambition, fed
by his few old books.

He read the familiar pages and realized again that the intellect had triumphed over the spirit, and both had conquered emotion. The men of Moon, at least, had become as barren as their accident of a planet.

Pepin knew much of Earth as his people's traders had described it. Knew that it was changing and was no longer as it was when his books were written. Yet still he yearned to go there and see if he could find some trace of what he needed—though he would only know what he needed when he found it.

For some time he had planned to visit Earth and his people were willing that he should go, if he did not return, for he discomfited them. His name—his true name—was on the list, close to the top. Soon a ship would be ready for him. His true name was P Karr.

Now he thought of the ship and decided to go to the list. He went to the list infrequently for in his atavism he was superstitous and believed completely that the more he looked at it, the less chance there would be of his name being at the top.

Pepin jerked his body off his stool and slammed the book shut. On the hushed world of Moon, he made as much noise as he could.

He limped, more evidently high-shouldered now that he was moving, towards the door section of his dome. He took down his helmet and fitted it on to his shoulders, activated the door section, and crossed the sharp, bright ground covering the distance between himself and the city. By choice, and to the relief of his people, he lived outside the city.

On the surface, there was little to see of the city. Merely a storey or two, perhaps three in places. All the prominences were square and transparent, to absorb as much energy from the waning sun as possible.

Another door section in one of the buildings opened to him and he went inside, hardly realizing that he had left the surface. He entered a funnel containing a disc-shaped platform and the platform began to fall downwards, slowing as it reached the bottom.

Here the light was completely artificial and the walls were of metal—plain, undecorated tubes twice the height of a tall, thin Moonite. Pepin was not typical of his race.

He limped along this tube for a short distance, until the floor began to move. He let it carry him through the laby-

rinthine intestines of the city until he came to the hall he
wanted.

The hall was quite unpopulated until Pepin entered. It had
a domed ceiling and was covered by screens, charts, indica-
tors, conveying every item of information which a citizen
might require to know in the day-to-day life of the city.
Pepin went to the list, craning his head to look at it. He
stared at the bottom and followed the list of names up.

His name was at the top. He must go immediately to Ship
Controller and apply for his ship. If he did not, his name
would go back to the bottom, according to regulations.

As he turned to leave the hall, another Moonite entered. His
helmet was flung back, lying against his shoulder blades. His
golden hair was long and his thin face smiled.

This was G Nak, the greatest of the trader pilots, and he
did not need to look at the list, for he had a permanent ship
of his own. The population of Moon was small, and G Nak
knew Pepin as well as anyone.

He stopped sharply, arms akimbo, and contemplated the
list.

"So you journey to Earth P Karr. You will find it decadent
and unpleasant. Take plenty of food—you will not like their
salty grub."

"Thank you," bobbed Pepin as he left.

As if mutated by their constant contact with the mother
planet, only the ships of Moon had character. They were burnished and patterned with fancifully wrought images. Ancient
animals prowled along their hulls, gargoyles glowered from
indentations created by heavily moulded figures of famous
men, tentacled hands curled themselves over the curves like
the arms of wrecked sailors clinging to spars, or else like the
protective hands of a she-baboon about her young. The ships
were so heavily decorated that in the light they looked like
frozen lava, all lumps and gulleys in obsidian or brass.

Pepin, luggage on back, paused before he put foot on the
short, moving ramp which would deliver him to the entrance
of his allotted ship. He allowed himself time to study the
raised images, then stepped upon the ramp and was whisked
up to the airlock which opened for him.

The inside of the ship was very cramped and consisted
mainly of cargo space. The cargo, which would go with

Pepin and be delivered to an Earth-city called Barbart, was already stowed. Pepin lowered himself on to the couch where he would spend the journey. After Pepin and cargo had been delivered, the ship would return, as it had left, automatically.

A whisper of noise, hushed like all Moon sounds, warned him that the ship was about to take-off. He braced himself; felt no sensation as the ship rose on course for Earth.

The bright ship sped through the soft darks of weary space, a bold spark intruding the blackness. It flickered along its path until at length Pepin's screen picked up the growing globe of Earth—brown, yellow and white, turning slowly in the scant warmth of the dormant sun.

The planet seemed vaguely unreal, perhaps because it was imperfectly focused on the screen, yet the stuff of space seemed to drift through it as if the planet's very fabric was worn thin. Pepin felt the hard metal rocket would not stop when it reached Earth, but tear through it easily and continue on into empty space where more vital stars pulsed. At one time, Pepin knew, the universe had been even thicker with bright stars, and even his own sun had possessed more than the three planets that now circled it.

Silently, the ship went into orbit, easing itself by stages into the atmosphere, down through the clear, purple sky, down into the brown cloud-banks that hung close to the ground, through the clouds until it had levelled out again and moved with decreasing speed across sluggish seas and wastes of dark yellow, brown and black, studded by great white patches of salt. Much further inland, grey moss became apparent, and later the waving light green of the fragile fronds that marked what Earth's inhabitants called the Land of Fronds. In the Land of Fronds were two principal cities, two towns and a village. Barbart, the trading port between Moon and Earth, lay in a gentle valley. The hills were covered in fronds that from above seemed like a rolling sea—more sea-like than the salt-heavy waters far to the east.

Barbart was laid out precisely, in quadrangles, triangles and star-shaped plazas. The roofs of the low houses were of dark green and brick-brown, yet seemed brightly coloured compared with their surroundings. The ship passed over the huge red-gold machine which rose high above the other buildings. This, Pepin knew, was called the Great Regulator and supplied necessary power to the city. Behind the Great Regulator, in the city's central plaza, was a cradlepad ready for his ship. It hovered and then dropped down on to the cradlepad.

Pepin shivered suddenly and did not rise immediately but watched his screen as people began to enter the plaza, moving speedily towards the ship.

Barbart was the city most like those he had read about in his books. It was considerably smaller than the Golden Age cities had been and resembled best a medieval Italian city. From the ground, even the frond-covered hills might be a forest of oaks and elms if they were not looked at closely. Also Pepin knew that the folk of Barbart were quite similar to the ancient folk of Earth. Yet he could not convince himself, though he tried, that he had returned to the Earth of his books. For one thing the light was fainter, the air darker, the drifting brown clouds unlike any that had existed in Earth's past. Pepin was not as disappointed as he expected. Whatever deficiencies existed here, at least the planet was *natural* and Pepin placed much value on the naturalness of things.

The airlock had opened and the Barbartians grouped themselves outside it, waiting for the pilot to appear.

Pepin took up his luggage from beside the couch, swung his well-shaped legs to the floor and limped out of the cabin and through the airlock.

The heavy, brine-laden air half-choked him. The smell of salt was so marked that he felt faintly sick. He swung his helmet up so that it enclosed his head. He turned on his emergency oxygen supply, deciding to give himself time to adjust.

The merchants of Barbart stood around the ramp leading from the cradlepad. They looked at him eagerly.

"May we inspect the cargo, Pilot?" enquired a heavy-shouldered man with broad cheek-bones and a flaking skin half-invisible beneath his thick, black beard. He wore a quilted coat, belted at his chest. This was a rusty black. A white stock was tied at his throat and he wore baggy yellow trousers tucked into furry boots.

Pepin looked at him, wanting to greet him in some manner that would convey the pleasure he felt at seeing a human-being of heavy build, with muscles and flaws on his skin.

"Pilot?" said the merchant.

Pepin began to limp slowly down the ramp. He stood aside to let the bulky merchant move up it and duck his head to enter the airlock. Three others followed him, glancing rather quizzically at the silent Moonite.

A man smaller than Pepin with the narrow face of a reptile, dressed in dull red and black, sidled up clutching a handwritten list. Fascinated, Pepin looked at it, not understanding the words. He would like to have taken off his gauntlets and fingered the parchment but he would wait for a little.

"Pilot? When do you return?"

Pepin smiled. "I do not return. I have come to live here."

The man was startled. He took the parchment back and turned his head, did not see what he looked for and gazed up the ramp towards the open airlock.

"Then be welcome," he said absently, still not looking at Pepin. He excused himself and walked with short, rapid steps back to the warehouse at the side of the plaza.

Pepin waited until the merchant and his friends reappeared. They looked satisfied and were nodding to one another. The black-bearded merchant bustled down the ramp and slapped Pepin's arm.

"I admit it," he grinned, "a very generous cargo. We have the best of this month's bargain I think. Gold and alcohol for our fertilizers. May I begin unloading?"

"As you wish," Pepin said courteously, wondering at this man who could delight in receiving such useless things in return for valuable fertilizers.

"You are new," said the merchant, taking Pepin's arm and leading him towards the warehouse where the other man had gone. "What do you think of our city?"

"It is wonderful," sighed Pepin. "I admire it. I should like to live here."

"Ha! Ha! With all those marvels and comforts in Moon you have. You'd miss them after a while, Pilot. And every year we hear of cities dying, populations shrinking, fewer children than ever being born. No, I envy you Moonites with your safety and stability—you don't have to worry about the future, for you can plan efficiently. But we here can make no plans—we merely hope that things will not alter too much in our own lifetimes."

"At least you are part of the natural order, sir," Pepin said hesitantly. "You might adapt further as the Earth changes."

The merchant laughed again. "No—we of Earth will all be dead. We accept this, now. The human race has had a long run. No one would have expected us to last this time, but soon the point will be reached where we can adapt no longer. It is already happening in less fortunate areas. Man is dying out on Earth. Yet while you have your System, that is not possible on Moon."

"But our System is artificial—your planet is natural."

They reached the warehouse. Men were already folding back the heavy doors. The casks of fertilizer were stacked in a cool, dark corner of the place. The man with the reptile face glanced at Pepin as he counted the casks.

"There is the matter of the pilot's gift," said the merchant. "The traditional gift of gratitude to the man who brings the cargo safely to us. Is there anything we have which you desire?"

Traditionally, the pilot asked for a small token gift of no great value and Pepin knew what was expected of him.

"You mine antiques in Barbart I believe?" he said politely.

"Yes. It provides employment for criminals. Forty cities have stood where Barbart now stands."

Pepin smiled with pleasure. Such history!

"I am fond of books," he said.

"Books?" The merchant frowned. "Why, yes, we have a stack of those somewhere. Have the folk of Moon taken to reading? Ha! ha!"

"You do not read them yourselves?"

"A lost art, Pilot. Those ancient languages are impossible. We have no scholars in Barbart, save for our elders—and their wisdom comes from here," he tapped his head, "not from any books. We've lttle use for the old knowledge—it was a knowledge suitable for a younger Earth."

Though Pepin understood, he felt a pang of sorrow and dissapointment. Intellectually he had known that the folk of Earth would not be like his idealized picture of them, yet emotionally he could not accept this.

"Then I would like some books," he said.

"As many as your ship has room for when our cargo's loaded!" promised the merchant. "What language do you read in? I'll let you sort them out for yourself."

"I read in all the ancient tongues," said Pepin proudly. His fellows thought his a useless skill and it probably was, but he did not care.

He added: "And there is no need to load them. I shall not be returning with the ship. That will go back to Moon automatically."

"You'll not be—? Are you then to be some sort of permanent representative of Moon on Earth?"

"No. I wish to live on Earth as one of her folk."

The merchant scratched his nose. "Aha, I see. Aha . . ."

"Is there reason why I should not be welcome."

"Oh, no—no—I was merely astonished that you should elect to stay with us. I gather you Moonites regard us as primitives, doomed to die with the planet." His tone was now mildly resentful. "Your regulation admitting no one of Earth to Moon have been strict for centuries. No Earthman has visited Moon, even. You have your stability to consider, of course. But why should you *elect* to suffer the discomforts of our wasted planet?"

"You will note," said Pepin carefully, "that I am not like other Moonites. I am, I suppose, some sort of romantic throwback—or it may be that my original difference has fostered mental differences, I do not know. However, I alone amongst my race have an admiration for Earth and the folk of Earth. I have a yearning for the past whereas my people look always to the future—a future which they are pledged to keep stable and as much like the present as possible."

"I see . . ." The merchant folded his arms. "Well, you are welcome to stay here as a guest—until you wish to return to Moon."

"I never wish to return."

"My friend," the merchant smiled. "You will wish to return soon enough. Spend a month with us—a year—but I warrant you'll stay no longer."

He paused before saying: "You'll find plenty of signs of the past here—for the past is all we have. There is no future for Earth."

The clock, centerpiece of the Great Regulator, had measured off six weeks before Pepin Hunchback became restless and frustrated by the uncaring ignorance of the Barbartians. The citizens were pleasant enough and treated him well considering their covert antipathy towards the Moonites. But he made no friends and found no sympathizers.

He rejoiced in those books which were not technical manuals or technical fiction. He enjoyed the poetry and the legends and the history books and the adventure stories. But there were fewer than he had expected and did not last him long.

He lived in a room at an Inn. He grew used to the heavy, briny air and the dull colours, he began to enjoy the gloom which shadowed the Earth, for it mirrored something of his own mood. He would go for walks over the hills and watch the heavy brown clouds course towards him from the horizon, smell the sweetish scent of the frond forests, climb the crumbling rocks that stood against the purple sky, worn by the wind and scoured by the salt.

Unlike Moon, this planet still lived, still held surprises in the sudden winds that blew its surface, the odd animals which crawled over it.

Pepin was afraid only of the animals, for these had become truly alien. The principal life-form other than man was the oozer—a giant leech which normally prowled the bleak sea shores but which was being seen increasingly further inland. If Man's time was ending, then the time of the oozer was beginning. As Man died out, the oozer multiplied. They moved in schools varying from a dozen to a hundred, depending on the species—they grew from two feet to ten feet long. Some were black, some brown, some yellow—but the most disgusting was the white variety which was also the largest and most ferocious, a great grub of a thing capable of fast speeds, able to outdistance a running man and bring him down. When this happened, the oozer, like its leech ancestor, fed off the blood only and left the body drained and dry.

Pepin saw a school moving through a glade once as he sat on a rock staring down into the frond forest.

"The new tenants," he said aloud, after he'd conquered his nausea, "are arriving—and the Earth ignores Man. She is not hostile, she is not friendly. She no longer supports him. She has forgotten him. Now she fosters new children."

Pepin was given to talking to himself. It was the only time when words came easily—when he was alone.

Pepin tried to talk with Kop, the merchant and his fellow residents at the Inn, but though they were polite enough, his questions, his statements and his arguments made them frown and puzzle and excuse themselves early.

One fellow resident, a mild-mannered and friendly man called Mokof, middle-aged with a slight stoop, made greater attempts to understand Pepin, but was incapable, rather than unwilling of helping him.

"With your talk of the past and philosophy, you would be

happier in that odd city of Lanjis Liho by the sea," he said pleasantly one day as they sat outside the Inn, tankards at their sides, watching the fountain play in the plaza.

Pepin had heard Lanjis Liho mentioned, but had been so curious about other matters, that he had not asked of the city before. Now he raised one fair, near-visible eyebrow.

"I once knew a man from Lanjis Liho," Mokof continued in answer. "He had a strange name which I forget—it was similar to your last name in type. He had a scar on his face. Got into trouble by eating his food at the wrong time, saved himself by fixing the Great Regulator for us. We know nothing of these machines these days. He believed that he could travel in Time, though I saw little evidence of this while he was here. All the folk of Lanjis Liho are like him, I hear—bizarre, if you follow me—they know nothing of clocks, for instance, have no means of measuring the hours. Their ruler is called Chronarch and he lives in a palace called the House of Time, though only an oozer knows why they should emphasize Time when they can't even *tell* it."

Mokof could tell Pepin very little more that was not merely opinion or speculation, but Lanjs Liho by the sea sounded an interesting place. Also Pepin was attracted by the words "time travel"—for his true wish was to return to Earth's past.

During the seventh week of his stay in Barbart, he decided to journey eastwards towards Lanjis Liho by the sea.

Pepin Hunchback set off on foot for Lanjis Liho. Mokof in particular tried to dissuade him—it was a long journey and the land was dangerous with oozers. He could easily lose his direction without a good steed.

But he had tried to ride the seal-beasts which were the mounts of most Earthmen. These creatures, with their strongly muscled forefins and razor-sharp tails, were reliable and fairly fast. They had built-up saddles of silicon to give the rider a straight seat. Part of their equipment also included a long gun, called a piercer, which fired a ray from its ruby core, and a torch fed by batteries which supplied the traveller with light in the moonless, near-starless night.

Pepin Hunchback took a torch and balanced a piercer over his shoulder. He liked the feeling both gave him. But he did not trust himself to a seal-beast.

He left in the dark morning, with food and a flask in the pack on his back, still dressed in his cloth-of-metal suit.

The citizens of Barbart, like those of Moon, were not regretful when he had gone. He had disturbed them when they
believed they had conquered all disturbances within themselves. For seven weeks he had interrupted their purpose and
the purpose they wished to transmit to any children they
might have.

That purpose was to die peacefully and generously on an
Earth which no longer desired their presence.

Pepin was disappointed as he limped away from Barbart in
the Land of Fronds. He had expected to find dynamic vitality
on Earth—people prepared for change, but not for death.
Somewhere on the planet—possibly in Lanjis Liho by the
sea—he would find heroes. From what Mokof had hinted, he
might even find a means of travelling into the past. This is
what he wanted most, but he had never expected to achieve
it.

The moss of the frond forests was springy and helped his
walking, but by evening it was beginning to give way to hard,
brown earth over which dust scurried. Ahead of him, ominous in the waning light, was a barren plain, cracked and almost featureless. Here and there chunks of rock stood up. He
selected one as his goal, realizing, even as night fell, cold and
pitch dark, that to sleep would be to risk his life. Oozers, he
had been told, only slept when they had fed—and there was
little to feed on save Man.

He pressed the grip of his torch and its light illuminated
a distance of a few yards around him. He continued to walk,
warm enough in his suit. As he walked, his mind became almost blank. He was so weary that he could not tell how long
he had marched by the degrees of weariness. But when a sil-
houette of rock became apparent in the torch-light, he
stopped, took off his pack, leant his back against the rock and
slid down it. He did not care about the oozers and he was
fortunate because no oozers scented his blood and came to
care about him.

Dawn came dark brown, the muddy clouds streaming
across the sky, blocking out much of the sun's dim light.
Pepin opened his pack and took out the flask of specially dis-
tilled fresh water. He could not drink the salt-water which the
folk of Earth drank. They, in turn, had adapted to the extent
where they could not bear to drink fresh water. He took two
tablets from a box and swallowed them. Having breakfasted,
he heaved his aching body up, adjusted the pack on his back,

slung the torch into its sheath at his side, shouldered the
piercer and looked about him.

In the west, the frond forests were out of sight and the
plain looked as endless in that direction as it did in the other.
Yet the plain to the east was now further broken by low hills
and many more rocks.

He set off eastwards. *In the east,* he reflected, *our ancestors
believed Paradise lay. Perhaps I will find my Paradise in the
east.*

If Paradise existed, and Pepin was entitled to enter, he
came very close to entering two days later as he collapsed
descending a salt-encrusted hill and rolled many feet down it,
knocking himself unconscious.

As it was, the Hooknosed Wanderer saved him from this
chance of Paradise.

The Hooknosed Wanderer was a burrower, a gossiper, a
quester after secrets. Amongst all the Earth folk he was perhaps the only aimless nomad. No one knew his origin, no one
thought to ask. He was as familiar in Barbart as he was in
Lanjis Liho. His knowledge of Earth, past and present, was
extensive but few ever availed themselves of it. He was a
short man with a huge nose, receding chin, and a close-fitting
hood and jerkin which made him resemble a beaked turtle.

He saw the fallen tangle that was Pepin Hunchback at
much the same time as the school of oozers scented Pepin's
blood.

He was riding a big fat seal-beast and leading another on
which was heaped a preposterous burden of rolled fabric, dig-
ging equipment, a small stove, angular bundles—in fact the
Hooknosed Wanderer's entire household tied precariously to
the seal-beast's back. The seal-beast seemed mildly pleased
with itself that it was capable of carrying this load.

In the Hooknosed Wanderer's right hand, borne like a
lance resting in a special grip on his stirrup, was his piercer.
He saw Pepin, he saw the oozers.

He rode closer, raised his piercer, pressed the charger and
then the trigger-stud. The concentrated light was scarcely visible but it bit into the oozer school instantaneously. They were
of the black variety. The Hooknosed Wanderer moved the
piercer about very gradually and burned every oozer to
death. It gave him satisfaction.

Then he rode up to where Pepin lay and looked down at

him. Pepin was not badly hurt, he was even beginning to stir on the ground. The Hooknosed Wanderer saw that he was a Moonite by his dress. He wondered where Pepin had got the piercer and torch which lay near him.

He dismounted and helped the Moonite to his feet. Pepin rubbed his head and looked rather nervously at the Hooknosed Wanderer.

"I fell down," he said.

"Just so," said the Hooknosed Wanderer. "Where is your spaceship? Has it crashed nearby?"

"I have no spaceship," Pepin explained. "I was journeying from Barbart, where I landed some seven weeks ago, to Lanjis Liho, which I am told lies close to the shores of the sea."

"You were foolish to go on foot," said the Wanderer. "It is still a long way."

He continued eagerly: "But you must guest with me and we will talk about Moon. I should be happy to add to my knowledge."

Pepin's head was aching. He was glad that this odd stranger had come upon him. He agreed willingly and even tried to help the Wanderer raise his tent.

When the tent was finally erected and the Wanderer's goods distributed about it, Pepin and he went inside.

The Wanderer offered him leg-fish and salt-water, but Pepin refused politely and swallowed his own food.

Then he told the Wanderer of his coming from Moon to Earth, of his stay in Barbart, of his frustration and disappointment, and of his ambition. The Wanderer listened, asking questions that showed he was more interested in Moon than Pepin.

Listlessly, Pepin replied to these questions and then asked one of his own.

"What do you know of Lanjis Liho, sir?"

"Everything but the most recent events," said the Wanderer with a smile. "Lanjis Liho is very ancient and has its origin in an experimental village where a philosopher tried to educate people to regard Time as they regard Matter—something that can be moved through, manipulated and so on. From this, the Chronarchy was formed and it became traditional in Lanjis Liho to investigate Time and little else. Perhaps by mutation, perhaps by the awakening of some power we have always possessed, a race of people exist in Lanjis Liho who can *move themselves through Time!*

"I had the good fortune to know the young man who first discovered this talent within himself and trained others in its use. A man called the Scar-faced Brooder—he is the present Chronarch."

"He can travel into the past?"

"And future, so I hear. Once the chronopathic talent is released in Man, he can move through Time at will."

"But the past," said Pepin excitedly. "We can journey back to Earth's Golden Age and not worry about natural death or artificial living. We can *do* things!"

"Um," said the Wanderer. "I share your love for the past, Pepin Hunchback—my tent is full of antiques I have excavated—but is it possible to return to the past? Would not that act change the future—for there is no record in our history of men from the future settling in the past?"

Pepin nodded. "It is a mystery—yet surely *one* man, who did not admit he was from the future, could settle in the past?"

The Hooknosed Wanderer smiled. "I see what you mean."

"I realize now," said Pepin seriously, "that I have little in common with either my own people or the folk of Earth. My only hope is to return to the past where I shall find the things I need to exist fully. I am a man out of my time."

"You are not the first. Earth's ancient history is full of such men."

"But I shall be the first, perhaps, able to find the Age which most suits him."

"Perhaps," said the Hooknosed Wanderer dubiously. "But your wishes are scarcely constructive."

"Are they not? What, then, has this Earth to offer mankind? We on Moon live an artificial life, turning year by year into machines less perfect than those which support us. And you here accept death passively—are only concerned with the business of facing extinction 'well'! My race will not be human within a century—yours will not exist. Are we to perish? Are the values of humanity to perish—have the strivings of the last million years been pointless? Is there no escape from Earth's evening? I will not accept that!"

"You are not logical, my friend," smiled the Wanderer. "You take the least positive line of all—by refusing to face the future—by your desire to return to the past. How will that benefit the rest of us?"

Pepin clutched his head. "Ah," he murmured. "Ah . . ."

The Hooknosed Wanderer continued. "I have no wish to survive the evening. You have seen something of the horrors which will multiply as Earth's evening turns to night."

Pepin did not reply. He had become inarticulate with emotion.

The Hooknosed Wanderer took him outside and pointed into the east. "That way lies Lanjis Liho and her chronopaths," he said. "I pity you, Pepin, for I think you will find no solution to your problem—and it *is* your problem, not humanity's."

Pepin limped from weariness as well as deformity. He limped along a beach. It was morning and the dull, red sun was rising slowly from the sea as he moved down the dark shore towards Lanjis Liho. It was cold.

Grey-brown mist hung over the sea and drifted towards the bleak landscape that was dominated by the solid black outline of cliffs to his right. The brown beach glistened with patches of hard salt and the salt-sluggish sea was motionless, for there was no longer a nearby moon to move it.

Pepin still considered his conversation with the strange Wanderer. Was this the end of Earth, or merely one phase in a cycle? Night must come—but would it be followed by a new day? If so, then perhaps the future was attractive. Yet the Earth had slowly destroyed the greater part of the human race. Would the rest die before the new morning?

Suddenly, Pepin slipped into a pool of thick water. He floundered in the clinging stuff, dragging himself back by clutching a spur of hardened salt, but the salt wouldn't bear his weight and he fell into the pool again. Finally he crawled back to dry land. Everything was crumbling or changing.

He continued along the shore more carefully. Leg-fish scuttled away as he approached. They sought the deeper shadow of the crags of rock which rose from the beach like jagged teeth, corroded by wind-borne salt. They hid and were silent and the whole shore was quiet. Pepin Hunchback found no peace of mind here, but the solitude seemed to absorb his tangled thoughts and eased his brain a little.

The disc of the sun took a long time to rise above the horizon, and brought little light with it, and even less warmth. He paused and turned to stare over the sea which changed from black to brown as the sun came up. He sighed and looked at the sun which caught his face in its dull glow and stained it a deep pink, bringing a look of radiance to his native pallor.

Later, he heard a sound which he first took to be the squawking of fighting leg-fish. Then he recognized it as a human voice. Without moving his head, he listened more intently.

Then he turned.

A tiny figure sat on a seal on the cliff above. Jutting upwards from it like a lance was the barrel of a long piercer. The figure was half-shadowed by the ruin of an ancient watch-tower and, as he looked, jerked at the reins impatiently, disappeared into the whole shadow and was gone.

Pepin frowned and wondered if this could be an enemy. He readied his own piercer.

Now the rider had descended the cliff and was nearing him. He heard the distant thwack of the beast's fins against the damp beach. He levelled the gun.

The rider was a woman. A woman from out of his books.

She was tall, long-legged, with the collar of her seal-leather jacket raised to frame her sharp-jawed face. Her brown hair drifted over it and flew behind. One hand, protected by a loose-fitting glove, clutched the pommel of her high, silicon saddle. The other held her beast's reins. Her wide, full-lipped mouth seemed pursed by the cold, for she held it tight.

Then her seal entered a deep pool of sluggish water and began swimming through it with great difficulty. The stong smell of the brine-thick liquid came to his awareness then and he saw her as a woman out of mythology—a mermaid astride a seal. Yet, she frightened him. She was unexpected.

Was she from Lanjis Liho? It was likely. And were they all like her?

Now, as she reached firm ground again, she bagan to laugh in rhythm with the seal's movement. It was rich, delightful laughter, but as she came towards him, the deavy drops of water rolling slowly from her mount, his stomach contracted in panic. He backed away a few paces.

At this moment she seemed to personify the bleak insanity of the dying planet.

She halted her beast close to him. She lowered her chin and opened her grey-green eyes. She still smiled.

"Stranger, you are from Moon by your garb. Are you lost?"

He put the piercer over his shoulder. "No. I seek Lanjis Liho."

She pointed backwards up the beach. "You are close to our city. I am Tall Laugher, sister to the Scar-faced Brooder, Chronarch of the City of Time. I will take you there."

"I am Pepin Hunchback, without kin or rank."

"Climb up on my seal-beast's back, hang on to my saddle and we will soon be in Lanjis Liho."

He obeyed her, clinging desperately to the slippery silicon as she wheeled the seal about and sped back the way she had come.

She called to him once or twice on the journey up the salty beach, but he could not make out the sense.

It had begun to rain a little before they reached Lanjis Liho.

Built upon a huge and heavy cliff, the city was smaller even than Barbart, but its houses were tower-like—slim and ancient with conical roofs and small windows. Lanjis Liho was dominated by the Tower of Time which rose from a building called, according to Tall Laugher's shouted description, the Hall of Time, palace of the Chronarch.

Both Hall and Tower were impressive, though puzzling. Their design was an impossibility of curves and angles, bright colours bordering on the indefinable, and creating an emotion in Pepin similar to the emotion created in him by pictures of Gothic architecture—though whereas Gothic took the mind soaring upwards, this took the mind in all directions.

The pale sun shone down on the city streets and the salt-rain fell, washing the gleaming salt deposits off the walls and roofs and leaving fresh ones. The drops even fell between the blades and domes of the Hall and Tower of Time.

There were few people in the streets, and yet there seemed to be an air of activity about the city—almost as if the people were preparing to abandon it.

Although quite similar in their various types to the fold of Barbart, these people seemed livelier—eager.

Pepin wondered if he had arrived at a festival time, as Tall Laugher reined in her beast on the corner of a narrow street. He clambered down, his bones throbbing. She also dismounted and pointed at the nearest house. "This is where I live. Since you claimed no rank, I gather you have come here as a visitor and not as an official emissary from Moon. What do you seek in Lanjis Liho?"

"Transport to the past," he said at once.

She paused. "Why should you want that?"

"I have nothing in common with the present."

She looked at him through her cool, intelligent eyes. Then she smiled. "There is nothing in the past that would attract you."

"Let me decide."

"Very well," she shrugged, "but how do you propose to find the past?"

"I," his momentary confidence disappeared, "I had hoped for your help."

"You will have to speak with the Chronarch."

"When?"

She looked at him, frowning slightly. She did not seem unsympathetic. "Come," she said, "we will go the the Hall of Time now."

As Pepin followed the girl, walking quickly to keep up with her long strides, he wondered if perhaps the people of Lanjis Liho were bent on keeping the secrets of Time to themselves.

Though they glanced at him curiously as they passed him, the citizens did not pause. The mood of hurried activity seemed even stronger as they reached the spiralling steps which led upwards to the great gates of the Hall.

The guards did not challenge them as they entered an echoing corridor, the tall walls of which were decorated with peculiar cryptographs inlaid in silver, bronze and platinum.

Ahead of them were double-doors of yellow gold. Tall Laugher pushed against these and they entered a large, oblong wall with a high ceiling. At the far end, on a dais, was a seated man talking to a couple of others who turned as Tall Laugher and Pepin Hunchback entered.

The seated man smiled calmly as he saw Tall Laugher. He murmured to the other two who left by a door at the side of the dais. The man's pale face bore a scar running from the left corner of his mouth along his cheek-bone. His black hair swept from a widow's peak to his wide shoulders. He wore clothes that did not suit him—evidently the clothes of his office. His shirt was of yellow cloth and his cravat, knotted high at his chin, was black. He wore a long-sleeved jacket of quilted blue velvet and breeches of wine-red. His feet were shod in black slippers.

The hall itself was strange. At regular intervals the walls were set alternately with symbolic mosaics and computers. Behind the seated man, close to the far wall, which was blank, was a metal bench bearing the ancient tools of alchemy. They seemed in bizarre contrast to the rest of the hall.

"Well, Tall Laugher," said the man, "who is this visitor?"

"He is from Moon, Brooder—and seeks to journey into the past!"

The Scar-faced Brooder, Chronarch of Lanjis Liho, laughed and then, looking sharply at Pepin, stopped.

Pepin said eagerly: "I have heard that you can travel in Time at will. This is true?"

"Yes," said the Brooder, "but . . ."

"Do you plan to go backward or forward?"

The Scar-faced Brooder seemed nonplussed. "Forward, I suppose—but what makes you think you have the ability for travelling in Time?"

"Ability?"

"It is a special skill—only the folk of Lanjis Liho possess it."

"Have you no *machines?*" Pepin demanded, his spirits sinking.

"We do not *need* machines. Our skill is natural."

"But I must return to the past—I *must!*" Pepin limped towards the dais, ignoring the restraining hand of the Tall Laugher. "You want no one else to share your chance of escape! You must know much about Time—you must know how to help me return to the past!"

"It would do you no good if you went back."

"How do you know?"

"We know," said the Chronarch bleakly. "My friend, give up this obsession. There is nothing we can do for you in Lanjis Liho."

"You are lying!" Pepin changed his tone and said more levelly: "I beg you to help me. I—I need the past as others need air to survive!"

"You speak from ignorance."

"What do you mean?"

"I mean that the secrets of Time are more complex than

you believe." The Chronarch stood up. "Now I must leave you. I have a mission in the future."

He frowned, as if concentrating—and vanished.

Pepin was startled. "Where has he gone?"

"Into the future—to join others of our folk. He will return soon, I hope. Come, Pepin Hunchback, I will take you to my house and let you eat and rest there. After that, if you'll accept my advice, you had best arrange to go back to Moon."

"You must be able to construct a machine!" he shouted. "There must be a way! I must return!"

"Return?" she said, raising an eyebrow. "Return? How can you return to somewhere you have never been? Come." She led the way out of the hall.

Pepin Hunchback had calmed down by the time he had eaten a little of the salty food in Tall Laugher's house. They sat in a small room with a bay window which overlooked the street. He sat on one side of a table, she on the other. He did not speak. His mood had become apathetic. She seemed sympathetic and he was attracted to her for the qualities which he had first noted on the beach, and for her warm womanliness, but his despair was greater. He stared at the table, his twisted body bent over it, his hands stretched out in front of him.

"Your yearning, Pepin Hunchback, is not for the past as it was," she was saying softly. "It is for a world that never existed—a Paradise, a Golden Age. Men have always spoken of such a time in history—but such an idyllic world is a yearning for childhood, not the past, for lost innocence. It is childhood we wish to return to."

He looked up and smiled bitterly. "My childhood was not idyllic," he said. "I was a mistake. My birth was an accident. I had no friends, no peace of mind."

"You had your wonderment, your illusion, your hopes. Even if you could return to Earth's past—you would not be happy."

"Earth's present is decadent. Here the decadence is part of the process of evolution, on Moon it is artificial, that is all. Earth's past was never truly decadent."

"One cannot recapture the past."

"An old saying—yet your ability disproves that."

"You do not know, Pepin Hunchback," she said almost sadly. "Even if you used the ship, you could not . . ."

"Ship?"

"A Time craft, an earlier, cruder experiment we abandoned. We have no need of such devices now."

"It still exists?"

"Yes—it stands behind the Hall of Time," she spoke vaguely, her thoughts on something else.

Afraid that she would soon guess what was in his mind, Pepin changed the subject.

"Maybe you are right, Tall Laugher. Old Earth had none to love her any longer—her appearance does not inspire love. If I am the last who loves Earth, then I should stay with her." Part of him meant what he said, he realized. The words had come spontaneously, he had never considered this before.

She had only half-heard his words. She gave him a slightly startled look as he spoke. She rose from the table. "I will show you to your room," she said. "You need sleep."

He pretended to agree and followed her out. There would be no sleep now. He must seize his opportunity. Outside, in the fading light of evening, lay a Time craft. Soon, perhaps, he could return to the past, to security, to a green, golden Earth, leaving this tired ball of salt forever!

There was enough light coming from the houses to show him the way through the twisting streets to the Tower of Time. He was unobserved as he circled around the great building, searching for the ship which Tall Laugher had said was there.

At last, half-seen in shadows, he noticed a shape lying in a small square at the back of the Tower.

Resting in davits was a ship of cold, blue metal. It could only be the Time craft. It was large enough to contain three or four men. Several other machines stood nearby, showing signs of neglect. Pepin limped cautiously forward until he stood by the ship. He touched it. It swayed slightly and the davits squealed. Pepin tried to steady it, looking nervously around him, but no one had noticed. The ship was roughly egg-shaped, with a small airlock in its side. Running his hand over it, Pepin found a stud which he pressed. The outer door slid open.

With considerable difficulty, Pepin managed to heave himself into the violently swinging ship. The noise of the squealing davits was ghastly. He shut the door and crouched in the utter blackness of the interior as it swayed back and forth.

It was likely that a light-stud was near the door. His searching hand found a projection and hesitated. Then, risking the possibility that it was not for the light, he pressed it.

The light came on. It was a bluish, mellow light, but it served adequately to show the interior of the ship. There were no seats and most of the machinery seemed hidden behind squat casings. At the centre of the ship was a column on which was set, at hand height, four controls. The ship was still swaying as Pepin went over to the controls and inspected them. His life on Moon had made him very familiar with all kinds of machinery, and he noted that the system of measurement was the same. The largest dial was in the middle. A division on the right was marked with a minus sign and on the left with a plus sign—obviously indicating past and future. Yet Pepin had expected such a control to be marked off with dates. There were none. Instead there were figures—units from one to ten. One trip, however, was all he would need in order to equate these numbers with the actual period of time they measured.

Another dial seemed to indicate speed. A switch was marked "Emergency Return" and another, mysteriously, "Megaflow Tuner".

Now all Pepin had to discover was whether the ship was still powered.

He limped over to another bank of instruments. There was a lever set into it. At the moment the indicator on its handle said OFF. His heart beating rapidly, Pepin pushed the lever down. A light flashed on the indicator and now it read ON. An almost inaudible humming came from the bank of instruments as needles swung and screens gleamed. Pepin returned to the column and put his large hand on the central dial. It moved easily to the right. He left it at —3.

The ship no longer swung on its davits. There was no sensation of speed, but the banks of instruments began to click and whirr noisily and Pepin felt suddenly dizzy.

The ship was moving backwards in Time.

Soon, he would be in the past at last!

Perhaps it was something to do with the ships' motion, the eruptions of colour which blossomed and faded on the screens, or the weird sounds of the instruments that made Pepin become almost hysterical. He began to laugh with joy. He had succeeded! His ambition was close to fruition!

At last the sounds died down, the sensation of sickness left him, the ship no longer seemed to move.

Pepin trembled as he raised his helmet and set it over his head. He knew enough to realize that the air of an earlier Earth would probably be too rich for him at first. This action saved his life.

He went to the door and pressed the stud to open it. The door moved backwards slowly and Pepin stepped into the airlock. The door closed. Pepin opened the outer door.

He looked out at absolutely nothing.

A lightless void lay around the ship. No stars, no planets—nothing at all.

Where was he? Had the ship's instruments been faulty? Had he been borne into an area of space so far away from any material body?

He felt vertigo seize him, backed into the airlock for as far as he could go, frightened that the vacuum would suck him into itself. He closed the outer door and returned to the ship.

In panic he went to the control column and again twisted the dial. This time to —8. Again the screens filled with colour, again lights blinked and needles swung, again he felt sick. Again the ship came to a stop.

More cautiously, he opened the inner door, closed it, opened the outer door.

Nothing.

Shouting inarticulately, he hurried back into the ship and turned the dial to —10. The same sensations. Another stop.

And outside was the same featureless pit of empty space.

There was only one thing left to do to test the ship. Set the dial for the future and see what lay there. If it was the same, he could switch to Emergency Return.

He swung the dial right round to +2.

The humming rose to a shrill. Lightning exploded on the screens, the needles sped around the dials and Pepin flung himself to the floor in panic as his head began to ache horribly. The ship seemed to be tossed from side to side and yet he remained in the same position on the floor.

At last the ship came to a halt. He got up slowly, passed through the airlock.

He saw *everything.*

He saw gold-flecked bands of blue spiralling away into infinity. He saw streamers of cerise and violet light. He saw heaving mountains of black and green. He saw clouds of orange and purple. Shapes formed and melted. It seemed he was a giant at one moment and a midget at the next. His mind was not equipped to take in so much.

Quickly, he shut the airlock.

What had he seen? A vision of chaos? The sight seemed to him to have been metaphysical rather than physical. But what had it signified? It had been the very opposite of the vacuum—it had been space filled with everything imaginable, or the components of everything. The ship could not be a Time craft after all, but a vessel for journeying—where? Another dimension? An alternate universe? But why the plus and minus signs on the controls? Why had Tall Laugher called this a Time ship? Had he been tricked?

He pushed back his helmet and wiped the sweat from his face. His eyes felt sore and his headache was worse. He was incapable of logical thought.

He was tempted to turn the dial marked "Emergency Return", but there was still the mysterious dial marked "Megaflow Tuner". Filled with hysterical recklessness, he turned it and was flung back as the ship jerked into normal motion. On the screens he saw a little of what he had observed outside.

All kinds of images appeared and disappeared. Once human figures—like golden shadows—were seen for a moment. His eyes fixed insanely on the screens, Pepin Hunchback could only stare.

Much, much later, he fell back to the floor. He had fainted.

At the sound of Tall Laugher's voice, he opened his eyes. His initial question was scarcely original, but it was the thing he most needed to know.

"Where am I?" he said, looking up at her.

"On the Megaflow," she replied. "You are a fool, Pepin Hunchback. The Brooder and I have had a considerable amount of difficulty locating you. It is a wonder you are not insane."

"I think I am. How did you get here?"

"We travelled up the Megaflow after you. But your speed was so great we wasted a great deal of energy catching you. I see from the instruments that you went into the past. Were you satisfied?"

He got up slowly. "Was that—that vacuum the *past*?"

"Yes."

"But it was not Earth's past?"

"It is the only past there is." She was at the controls, manipulating them. He turned his head and saw the Chronarch standing, head bowed, at the back of the ship.

He looked up and pursed his lips at Pepin.

"I attempted to explain—but I knew you would not believe me. It is a pity that you know the truth, for it will not console you, my friend."

"What *truth*?"

The Scar-faced Brooder sighed. He spread his hands. "The only truth there is. The past is nothing but limbo—the future is what you have observed—chaos, save for the Megaflow."

"You mean Earth only has existence in the *present*?"

"As far as we are concerned, yes." The Brooder folded his arms across his chest. "It means little to us of Lanjis Liho—but I knew how it would affect you. We are Time Dwellers, you see—you are still a Space Dweller. Your mind is not adjusted to understand and exist in the dimensions of Time-without-space."

"Time without space is an impossibility!" Pepin shouted.

The Brooder grimaced. "Is it? Then what do you think of the future—of the Megaflow? Admittedly something exists here, but it is not the stuff of space as you would understand it. It is—well, the physical manifestation of Time-without-space." He sighed as he noted Pepin's expression. "You will never properly understand, my friend."

Tall Laugher spoke. "We are nearly at Present, Brooder."

"I will explain further when we return to Earth," said the Chronarch kindly. "You have my sympathy, Pepin Hunchback."

In the Hall of Time, the scar-faced Brooder walked up to his dais and lowered himself into his chair. "Sit down, Pepin," he said, indicating the edge of the dais. Dazedly, Pepin obeyed.

"What do you think of the past?" said the Chronarch ironically, as Tall Laugher joined them. Pepin looked up at her and then at her brother. He shook his head.

Tall Laugher put her hand on his shoulder. "Poor Pepin . . ."

He did not have enough emotion left to feel anything at this. He rubbed his face and stared at the floor. His eyes were full of tears.

"Do you want the Chronarch to explain, Pepin?" she

asked. Looking into her face, he saw that she, too, seemed extraordinarily sad. Somehow she could understand his hopelessness. If only she were normal, he thought, and we had met in different circumstances. Even here, life would be more than bearable with her. He had never seen such a look of sympathy directed at him before. She was repeating her question. He nodded.

"At first we were as astonished as you at the true nature of Time," said the Chronarch. "But, of course, it was much easier for us to accept it. We are capable of moving through Time as others move through space. Time is now our natural element. We have adapted in a peculiar way—we are able to journey into the past or future merely by an effort of will. We have reached the stage where we no longer need space to exist. In Time-with-space our physical requirements are manifold and increasingly hard to meet on this changing planet. But in Time-without-space these physical requirements no longer exist."

"Brooder," put in Tall Laugher, "I do not think he is interested in us. Tell him why he found only limbo in the past."

"Yes," said Pepin, turning to stare at the Chronarch. "Tell me."

"I'll try. Imagine Time as a straight line along which the physical universe is moving. At a certain point on that line the physical universe exists. But if we move away from the present, backward or forward, what do we find?"

Again Pepin shook his head.

"We find what you found—for by leaving the present, we also leave the physical universe. You see, Pepin, when we leave our native Time stream, we move into others which are, in relation to us, *above* Time. There is a central stream along which our universe moves—we call this the Megaflow. As it moves it absorbs the stuff of Time—absorbs the chronons, as we call them, but leaves nothing behind. Chronons constitute the future—they are infinite. The reason you found nothing in the past is because, in a sense, space *eats* the chronons but cannot replace them."

"You mean Earth absorbs this—this temporal energy but emits none herself—like a beast prowling through Time gobbling it up but excreting nothing." Pepin spoke with a faint return of interest. "Yes, I understand."

The Chronarch leaned back. "So when you came to me

asking to return to the past, I almost told you this, but you would not have believed me. You did not want to. You cannot return to Earth's past because, simply, it no longer exists. Neither is there a future in terms of space, only in terms of the chronon-constituted Megaflow and its offshoots. We have managed to move ourselves where we wish, individually absorbing the chronons we need. Thus, the human race will continue—possibly we shall be immortal, ranging the continents of Time at will, exploring, acquiring knowledge which will be useful to us."

"While the rest of us die or turn into little better than machines," said Pepin flatly.

"Yes."

"Now I have no hope at all," said Pepin, rising. He limped up to Tall Laugher. "When do you leave for good?"

"Shortly."

"I thank you for your sympathy and courtesy," he said.

He left them standing silently in the Hall of Time.

Pepin walked along the beach, still moving towards the east, away from Lanjis Liho by the sea. The morning was a brown shroud covering the endlessness of sluggish sea and salt-frosted land, illuminated by a dying sun, blown by a cold wind.

Ah, he thought, *this is a morning for tears and self-contempt. Loneliness sits upon me like a great oozer with its mouth at my throat, sucking me dry of optimism. If only I could give myself up to this pitiless morning, let it engulf me, freeze me, toss me on its frigid wind and sink me in its slow-yielding sea, to lose sight of sun and sky, such as they are, and return to Mother Earth's ever-greedy womb . . .*

Oh, this alien Earth!

And yet he did not envy the Time Dwellers. Like the Moonites, they were renouncing their humanity. At least he still had his.

He turned as he heard his name called—a thin cry like that of an ancient seabird.

Tall Laugher was riding towards him, waving to him. She rode beneath the brown and heaving sky, her back straight and a smile on her lips and for some reason it seemed to him that she was riding to him out of the past, as when he had first seen her, a goddess from an age of mythology.

The red disc of the sun glowed behind her and again he noticed the strong smell of brine.

He waited by the edge of the thick, salt sea and, as he waited, he knew that his journey had been worth while.

The Deep Fix

One

Quickening sounds in the early dusk. Beat of hearts, surge of blood.

Seward turned his head on the bed and looked towards the window. They were coming again. He raised his drug-wasted body and lowered his feet to the floor. He felt nausea sweep up and through him. Dizzily, he stumbled towards the window, parted the blind and stared out over the white ruins.

The sea splashed far away, down by the harbour, and the mob was again rushing through the broken streets towards the Research Lab. They were raggedly dressed and raggedly organized, their faces were thin and contorted with madness, but they were numerous.

Seward decided to activate the Towers once more. He walked shakily to the steel-lined room on his left. He reached out a grey, trembling hand and flicked down three switches on a bank of hundreds. Lights blinked on the board above the switches. Seward walked over to the monitor-computer and spoke to it. His voice was harsh, tired and cracking.

"GREEN 9/7—0 Frequency. RED 8/5—B Frequency." He didn't bother with the other Towers. Two were enough to deal with the mob outside. Two wouldn't harm anybody too badly.

He walked back into the other room and parted the blind again. He saw the mob pause and look towards the roof where the Towers GREEN 9/7 and RED 8/5 were already beginning to spin. Once their gaze had been fixed on the Towers, they couldn't get it away. A few saw their companions look up and these automatically shut their eyes and dropped to the ground. But the others were now held completely rigid.

One by one, then many at a time, those who stared at the Towers began to jerk and thresh, eyes rolling, foaming at the mouth, screaming (he heard their screams faintly)—exhibiting every sign of an advanced epileptic fit.

Seward leaned against the wall feeling sick. Outside, those who'd escaped were crawling round and inching down the street on their bellies. Then, eyes averted from the Towers, they rose to their feet and began to run away through the ruins.

"Saved again," he thought bitterly.

What was the point? Could he bring himself to go on activating the Towers every time? Wouldn't there come a day when he would let the mob get into the laboratory, search him out, kill him, smash his equipment? He deserved it, after all. The world was in ruins because of him, because of the Towers and the other Hallucinomats which he'd perfected. The mob wanted its revenge. It was fair.

Yet, while he lived, there might be a way of saving something from the wreckage he had made of mankind's minds. The mobs were not seriously hurt by the Towers. It had been the other machines which had created the real damage. Machines like the Paramats, Schizomats, Engramoscopes, even Michelson's Stroboscope Type 8. A range of instruments which had been designed to help the world and had, instead, virtually destroyed civilization.

The memory was all too clear. He wished it wasn't. Having lost track of time almost from the beginning of the disaster, he had no idea how long this had been going on. A year, maybe? His life had become divided into two sections: drug-stimulated working-period; exhausted, troubled, tranquillized sleeping-period. Sometimes, when the mobs saw the inactive Towers and charged towards the laboratory, he had to protect himself. He had learned to sense the coming of a mob. They never came individually. Mob hysteria had become the universal condition of mankind—for all except Seward who had created it.

Hallucinomatics, neural stimulators, mechanical psycho-simulatory devices, hallucinogenic drugs and machines, all had been developed to perfection at the Hampton Research Laboratory under the brilliant direction of Prof. Lee W. Seward (33), psychophysicist extraordinary, one of the youngest pioneers in the field of hallucinogenic research.

Better for the world if he hadn't been, thought Seward wearily as he lowered his worn-out body into the chair and stared at the table full of notebooks and loose sheets of paper on which he'd been working ever since the result of Experiment Restoration.

Experiment Restoration. A fine name. Fine ideals to inspire it. Fine brains to make it. But something had gone wrong.

Originally developed to help in the work of curing mental disorders of all kinds, whether slight or extreme, the Hallucinomats had been an extension on the old hallucinogenic drugs such as CO_2, Mescalin and Lysergic Acid derivatives. Their immediate ancestor was the stroboscope and machines like it. The stoboscope, spinning rapidly, flashing brightly coloured patterns into the eyes of a subject, often inducing epilepsy or a similar disorder: the research of Burroughs and his followers into the early types of crude hallucinomats, had all helped to contribute to a better understanding of mental disorders.

But, as research continued, so did the incidence of mental illness rise rapidly throughout the world.

The Hampton Research Laboratory and others like it were formed to combat that rise with what had hitherto been considered near-useless experiments in the field of Hallucinomatics. Seward, who had been stressing the potential importance of his chosen field since university, came into his own. He was made Director of the Hampton Lab.

People had earlier thought of Seward as a crank and of the hallucinomats as being at best toys and at worse "madness machines," irresponsibly created by a madman.

But psychiatrists especially trained to work with them had found them invaluable aids to their studies of mental disorders. It had become possible for a trained psychiatrist to induce in himself a temporary state of mental abnormality by use of these machines. Thus he was better able to understand and help his patients. By different methods—light, soundwaves, simulated brain-waves, and so on—the machines created the symptoms of dozens of basic abnormalities and thousands of permutations. They became an essential part of modern psychiatry.

The result: hundreds and hundreds of patients, hitherto virtually incurable, had been cured completely.

But the birth-rate was rising even faster than had been predicted in the middle part of the century. And mental illness rose faster than the birth-rate. Hundreds of cases could be cured. But there were millions to be cured. There was no mass-treatment for mental illness.

Not yet.

Work at the Hamptom Research Lab became a frantic race to get ahead of the increase. Nobody slept much as, in the great big world outside, individual victims of mental illness turned into groups of—the world had only recently forgotten the old word and now remembered it again—*maniacs.*

An overcrowded, over-pressured world, living on its nerves, cracked up.

The majority of people, of course, did not succumb to total madness. But those who did became a terrible problem.

Governments, threatened by anarchy, were forced to re-institute the cruel, old laws in order to combat the threat. All over the world prisons, hospitals, mental homes, institutions of many kinds, all were turned into Bedlams. This hardly solved the problem. Soon, if the rise continued, the sane would be in a minority.

A dark tide of madness, far worse even than that which had swept Europe in the Middle Ages, threatened to submerge civilization.

Work at the Hampton Research Laboratory speeded up and speeded up—and members of the team began to crack. Not all these cases were noticeable to the over-worked men who remained sane. They were too busy with their frantic experiments.

Only Lee Seward and a small group of assistants kept going, making increasing use of stimulant-drugs and depressant-drugs to do so.

But, now that Seward thought back, they had not been sane, they had not remained cool and efficient any more than the others. They had seemed to, that was all. Perhaps the drugs had deceived them.

The fact was, they had panicked—though the signs of panic had been hidden, even to themselves, under the disciplined guise of sober thinking.

Their work on tranquillizing machines had not kept up with their perfection of simulatory devices. This was because they had had to study the reasons for mental abnormalities before they could begin to devise machines for curing them.

Soon, they decided, the whole world would be mad, well before they could perfect their tranquilomatic machines. They could see no way of speeding up this work any more.

Seward was the first to put it to his team. He remembered his words.

"Gentlemen, as you know, our work on hallucinomats for the actual *curing* of mental disorders is going too slowly. There is no sign of out perfecting such machines in the near future. I have an alternative proposal."

The alternative proposal had been Experiment Restoration. The title, now Seward thought about it, had been euphemistic. It should have been called Experiment Diversion. The existing hallucinomats would be set up throughout the world and used to induce *passive* disorders in the minds of the greater part of the human race. The co-operation of national governments and World Council was sought and given. The machines were set up secretly at key points all over the globe.

They began to "send" the depressive symptoms of various disorders. They worked. People became quiet and passive. A large number went into catatonic states. Others—a great many others, who were potentially inclined to melancholia, manic-depression, certain kinds of schizophrenia—committed suicide. Rivers became clogged with corpses, roads awash with blood and flesh of those who'd thrown themselves in front of cars. Every time a plane or rocket was seen in the sky, people expected to see at least one body come falling from it. Often, whole cargoes of people, were killed by the suicide of a captain, driver or pilot of a vehicle.

Even Seward had not suspected the extent of the potential suicides. He was shocked. So was his team.

So were the World Council and the national governments. They told Seward and his team to turn off their machines and reverse the damage they had done, as much as possible.

Seward had warned them of the possible result of doing this. He had been ignored. His machines had been confiscated and the World Council had put untrained or ill-trained operators on them. This was one of the last acts of the World

Council. It was one of the last rational—however ill-judged—acts the world knew.

The real disaster had come about when the bungling operators that the World Council had chosen set the hallucinomats to send the full effects of the conditions they'd originally been designed to produce. The operators may have been fools—they were probably mad themselves to do what they did. Seward couldn't know. Most of them had been killed by bands of psychopathic murderers who killed their victims by the hundreds in weird and horrible rites which seemed to mirror those of pre-history—or those of the insane South American cultures before the Spaniards.

Chaos had come swiftly—the chaos that now existed.

Seward and his three remaining assistants had protected themselves the only way they could, by erecting the stroboscopic Towers on the roof of the laboratory building. This kept the mobs off. But it did not help their consciences. One by one Seward's assistants had committed suicide.

Only Seward, keeping himself alive on a series of ever-more-potent drugs, somehow retained his sanity. And, he thought ironically, this sanity was only comparitive.

A hypodermic syringe lay on the table and beside it a small bottle marked M-A 19—Mescalin-Andrenol Nineteen—a drug hitherto only tested on animals, never on human beings. But all the other drugs he had used to keep himself going had either run out or now had poor effects. The M-A 19 was his last hope of being able to continue his work on the tranquilomats he needed to perfect and thus rectify his mistake in the only way he could.

As he reached for the bottle and the hypodermic, he thought coolly that, now he looked back, the whole world had been suffering from insanity well before he had even considered Experiment Restoration. The decision to make the experiment had been just another symptom of the world-disease. Something like it would have happened sooner or later, whether by natural or artificial means. It wasn't really his fault. He had been nothing much more than fate's tool.

But logic didn't help. In a way it *was* his fault. By now, with an efficient team, he might have been able to have constructed a few experimental tranquilomats, at least.

"Now I've got to do it alone," he thought as he pulled up his trouser leg and sought a vein he could use in his clammy, grey flesh. He had long since given up dabbing the area with anaesthetic. He found a blue vein, depressed the plunger of the needle and sat back in his chair to await results.

Two

They came suddenly and were drastic.

His brain and body exploded in a torrent of mingled ecstasy and pain which surged through him. Waves of pale light flickered. Rich darkness followed. He rode a ferris-wheel of erupting sensations and emotions. He fell down a never-ending slope of obsidian rock surrounded by clouds of green, purple, yellow, black. The rock vanished, but he continued to fall.

Then there was the smell of disease and corruption in his nostrils, but even that passed and he was standing up.

World of phosphorescence drifting like golden spheres into black night. Green, blue, red explosions. Towers rotate slowly. Towers Advance. Towers Recede. Advance, Recede. Vanish.

Flickering world of phosphorescent tears falling into the timeless, spaceless wastes of Nowhere. World of Misery. World of Antagonism. World of Guilt—guilt—guilt . . .

World of hateful wonder.

Heart throbbing, mind thudding, body shuddering as M-A 19 flowed up the infinity of the spine. Shot into back-brain, shot into mid-brain, shot into fore-brain.

EXPLOSION ALL CENTRES!

No-mind—No-body—No-where.

Dying waves of light danced out of his eyes and away through the dark world. Everything was dying. Cells, sinews, nerves, synapses—all crumbling. Tears of light, fading, fading.

Brilliant rockets streaking into the sky, exploding all together and sending their multicoloured globes of light—balls on a Xmas Tree—balls on a great tree—x-mass—drifting slowly earthwards.

Ahead of him was a tall, blocky building constructed of huge chunks of yellowed granite, like a fortress. Black mist swirled around it and across the bleak, horizonless nightscape.

This was no normal hallucinatory experience. Seward felt the ground under his feet, the warm air on his face, the half-familiar smells. He had no doubt that he had entered another world.

But where was it? How had he got here?

Who had brought him here?

The answer might lie in the fortress ahead. He began to walk towards it. Gravity seemed lighter, for he walked with greater ease than normal and was soon standing looking up at the huge green metallic door. He bunched his fist and rapped on it.

Echoes boomed through numerous corridors and were absorbed in the heart of the fortress.

Seward waited as the door was slowly opened.

A man who so closely resembled the Laughing Cavalier of the painting that he must have modelled his beard and clothes on it, bowed slightly and said:

"Welcome home, Professor Seward. We've been expecting you."

The bizarrely dressed man stepped aside and allowed him to pass into a dark corridor.

"Expecting me," said Seward. "How?"

The Cavalier replied good-humoredly: "That's not for me to explain. Here we go—through this door and up this corridor." He opened the door and turned into another corridor and Seward followed him.

They opened innumerable doors and walked along innumerable corridors.

The complexities of the corridors seemed somehow familiar to Seward. He felt disturbed by them, but the possibility of an explanation overrode his qualms and he willingly followed the Laughing Cavalier deeper and deeper into the fortress, through the twists and turns until they arrived at a door which was probably very close to the centre of the fortress.

The Cavalier knocked confidently on the door, but spoke deferentially. "Professor Seward is here at last, sir."

A light, cultured voice said from the other side of the door: "Good. Send him in."

This door opened so slowly that it seemed to Seward that he was watching a film slowed-down to a fraction of its proper speed. When it had opened sufficiently to let him enter, he went into the room beyond. The Cavalier didn't follow him.

It only occurred to him then that he might be in some kind of mental institution, which would explain the fortress-like nature of the building and the man dressed up like the Laughing Cavalier. But if so, how had he got here—unless he had collapsed and order had been restored sufficiently for someone to have come and collected him. No, the idea was weak.

The room he entered was full of rich, dark colours. Satin screens and hangings obscured much of it. The ceiling was not visible. Neither was the source of the rather dim light. In the centre of the room stood a dais, raised perhaps a foot from the floor. On the dais was an old leather armchair.

In the armchair sat a naked man with a cool, blue skin.

He stood up as Seward entered. He smiled charmingly and stepped off the dais, advancing towards Seward with his right hand extended.

"Good to see you, old boy!" he said heartily.

Dazed, Seward clasped the offered hand and felt his whole arm tingle as if it had had a mild electric shock. The man's strange flesh was firm, but seemed to itch under Seward's palm.

The man was short—little over five feet tall. His eyebrows met in the centre and his shiny black hair grew to a widow's peak.

Also, he had no navel.

"I'm glad you could get here, Seward," he said, walking back to his dais and sitting in the armchair. He rested his head in one hand, his elbow on the arm of the chair.

Seward did not like to appear ungracious, but he was worried and mystified. "I don't know where this place is," he said. "I don't even know how I get here—unless . . ."

"Ah, yes—the drug. M-A 19, isn't it? That helped, doubtless. We've been trying to get in touch with you for ages, old boy."

"I've got work to do—back there," Seward said obsessionally. "I'm sorry, but I want to get back as soon as I can. What do you want?"

The Man Without A Navel sighed. "I'm sorry, too, Seward. But we can't let you go yet. There's something I'd like to ask you—a favour. That was why we were hoping you'd come."

"What's your problem?" Seward's sense of unreality, never very strong here for, in spite of the world's bizarre appearance, it seemed familiar, was growing weaker. If he could help the man and get back to continue his research, he would.

"Well," smiled the Man Without A Navel, "it's really your problem as much as ours. You see," he shrugged diffidently, "we want your world destroyed."

"What!" Now something was clear, at last. This man and his kind did belong to another world—whether in space, time, or different dimensions—and they were enemies of Earth. "You can't expect me to help you do that!" He laughed. "You *are* joking."

The Man Without A Navel shook his head seriously. "Afraid not, old boy."

"That's why you want me here—you've seen the chaos in the world and you want to take advantage of it—you want me to be a—a fifth columnist."

"Ah, you remember the old term, eh? Yes, I suppose that is what I mean. I want you to be our agent. Those machines of yours could be modified to make those who are left turn against each other even more than at present. Eh?"

"You must be very stupid if you think I'll do that," Seward said tiredly. "I can't help you. I'm trying to help *them*." Was he trapped here for good? He said weakly: "You've got to let me go back."

"Not as easy as that, old boy. I—and my friends—want to enter your world, but we can't until you've pumped up your machines to such a pitch that the entire world is maddened and destroys itself, d'you see?"

"Certainly," exclaimed Seward. "But I'm having no part of it!"

Again the Man Without A Navel smiled, slowly. "You'll weaken soon enough, old boy."

"Don't be so sure," Seward said defiantly. "I've had plenty of chances of giving up—back there. I could have weakened. But I didn't."

"Ah, but you've forgotten the new factor, Seward."

"What's that?"

"The M-A 19."

"What do you mean?"

"You'll know soon enough."

"Look—I want to get out of this place. You can't keep me—there's no point—I won't agree to your plan. Where is this world, anyway?"

"Knowing that depends on you, old boy," the man's tone was mocking. "Entirely on you. A lot depends on you, Seward."

"I know."

The Man Without A Navel lifted his head and called: "Brother Sebastian, are you available?" He glanced back at Seward with an ironical smile. "Brother Sebastian may be of some help."

Seward saw the wall-hangings on the other side of the room move. Then, from behind a screen on which was painted a weird, surrealistic scene, a tall, cowled figure emerged, face in shadows, hands folded in sleeves. A monk.

"Yes, sir," said the monk in a cold, malicious voice.

"Brother Sebastian, Professor Seward here is not quite as ready to comply with our wishes as we had hoped. Can you influence him in any way?"

"Possibly, sir." Now the tone held a note of anticipation.

"Good. Professor Seward, will you go with Brother Sebastian?"

"No." Seward had thought the room contained only one door—the one he'd entered through. But now there was a chance of there being more doors—other than the one through which the cowled monk had come. The two men didn't seem to hear his negative reply. They remained where they were, not moving. "No," he said again, his voice rising. "What right have you to do this?"

"Rights? A strange question." The monk chuckled to himself. It was a sound like ice tumbling into a cold glass.

"Yes—rights. You must have some sort of organization here. Therefore you must have a ruler—or government. I demand to be taken to someone in authority."

"But I am in authority here, old boy," purred the blue-skinned man. "And—in a sense—so are you. If you agreed with my suggestion, you could hold tremendous power. Tremendous."

"I don't want to discuss that again." Seward began to walk towards the wall-hangings. They merely watched him—the monk with his face in shadow—the Man Without A Navel with a supercilious smile on his thin lips. He walked around a screen, parted the hangings—and there they were on the other side. He went through the hangings. This was some carefully planned trick—an illusion—deliberately intended to confuse him. He was used to such methods, even though he didn't understand how they'd worked this one. He said: "Clever—but tricks of this kind won't make me weaken."

"What on earth d'you mean, Seward, old man? Now, I wonder if you'll accompany Brother Sebastian here. I have an awful lot of work to catch up on."

"All right," Seward said. "All right, I will." Perhaps on the way to wherever the monk was going, he would find an opportunity to escape.

The monk turned and Seward followed him. He did not look at the Man Without A Navel as he passed his ridiculous dais, with its ridiculous leather armchair.

They passed through a narrow doorway behind a curtain and were once again in the complex series of passages. The tall monk—now he was close to him, Seward estimated his height as about six feet, seven inches—seemed to flow along in front of him. He began to dawdle. The monk didn't look back. Seward increased the distance between them. Still, the monk didn't appear to notice.

Seward turned and ran.

They had met nobody on their journey through the corridors. He hoped he could find a door leading out of the fortress before someone spotted him. There was no cry from behind him.

But as he ran, the passages got darker and darker until he was careering through pitch blackness, sweating, panting and beginning to panic. He kept blundering into damp walls and running on.

It was only much later that he began to realize he was running in a circle that was getting tighter and tighter until he was doing little more than spin round, like a top. He stopped, then.

These people evidently had more powers than he had suspected. Possibly they had some means of shifting the position of the corridor walls, following his movements by means of hidden TV cameras or something like them. Simply because there were no visible signs of an advanced technology didn't mean that they did not possess one. They obviously did. How else could they have got him from his own world to this?

He took a pace forward. Did he sense the walls drawing back? He wasn't sure. The whole thing reminded him vaguely of *The Pit and The Pendulum*.

He strode forward a number of paces and saw a light ahead of him. He walked towards it, turned into a dimly-lit corridor.

The monk was waiting for him.

"We missed each other, Professor Seward. I see you managed to precede me." The monk's face was still invisible, secret in its cowl. As secret as his cold mocking, malevolent voice. "We are almost there, now," said the monk.

Seward stepped towards him, hoping to see his face, but it was impossible. The monk glided past him. "Follow me, please."

For the moment, until he could work out how the fortress worked, Seward decided to accompany the monk.

They came to a heavy, iron-studded door—quite unlike any of the other doors.

They walked into a low-ceilinged chamber. It was very hot. Smoke hung in the still air of the room. It poured from a glowing brazier at the extreme end. Two men stood by the brazier.

One of them was a thin man with a huge, bulging stomach over which his long, narrow hands were folded. He had a shaggy mane of dirty white hair, his cheeks were sunken and his nose extremely long and extremely pointed. He seemed toothless and his puckered lips were shaped in a senseless smile—like the smile of a madman Seward had once had to experiment on. He wore a stained white jacket buttoned over his grotesque paunch. On his legs were loose khaki trousers.

His companion was also thin, though lacking the stomach. He was taller and had the face of a mournful bloodhound, with sparse, highly-greased, black hair that covered his bony head like a skull-cap. He stared into the brazier, not looking up as Brother Sebastian led Seward into the room and closed the door.

The thin man with the stomach, however, pranced forward, his hands still clasped on his paunch, and bowed to them both.

"Work for us, Brother Sebastian?" he said, nodding at Seward.

"We require a straight forward 'Yes,'" Brother Sebastian said. "You have merely to ask the question 'Will You?' If he replies 'No,' you are to continue. If he replies 'Yes,' you are to cease and inform me immediately."

"Very well, Brother. Rely on us."

"I hope I can." The monk chuckled again. "You are now in the charge of these men, professor. If you decide you want to help us, after all, you have only to say 'Yes.' Is that clear?"

Seward began to tremble with horror. He had suddenly realized what this place was.

"Now look here," he said. "You can't . . ."

He walked towards the monk who had turned and was opening the door. He grasped the man's shoulder. His hand seemed to clutch a delicate, bird-like structure. "Hey! I don't think you're a man at all. What *are* you?"

"A man or a mouse," chuckled the monk as the two grotesque creatures leapt forward suddenly and twisted Seward's arms behind him. Seward kicked back at them with his heels, squirmed in their grasp, but he might have been held by steel bands. He shouted incoherently at the monk as he shut the door behind him with a whisk of his habit.

The pair flung him on to the damp, hot stones of the floor. It smelt awful. He rolled over and sat up. They stood over him. The hound-faced man had his arms folded. The thin man with the stomach had his long hands on his paunch again. They seemed to rest there whenever he was not actually using them. It was the latter who smiled with his twisting, puckered lips, cocking his head to one side.

"What do *you* think, Mr Morl?" he asked his companion.

"I don't know, Mr Hand. After you." The hound-faced man spoke in a melancholy whisper.

"I would suggest Treatment H. Simple to operate, less work for us, a tried and trusty operation which works with most and will probably work with this gentleman."

Seward scrambled up and tried to push past them, making for the door. Again they seized him expertly and dragged him back. He felt the rough touch of rope on his wrists and the pain as a knot was tightened. He shouted, more in anger than agony, more in terror than either.

They were going to torture him. He knew it.

When they had tied his hands, they took the rope and tied his ankles. They twisted the rope up around his calves and under his legs. They made a halter of the rest and looped it over his neck so that he had to bend almost double if he was not to strangle.

Then they sat him on a chair.

Mr Hand removed his hands from his paunch, reached up above Seward's head and turned on the tap.

The first drop of water fell directly on the centre of his head some five minutes later.

Twenty-seven drops of water later, Seward was raving and screaming. Yet every time he tried to jerk his head away, the halter threatened to strangle him and the jolly Mr Hand and the mournful Mr Morl were there to straighten him up again.

Thirty drops of water after that, Seward's brain began to throb and he opened his eyes to see that the chamber had vanished.

In its place was a huge comet, a fireball dominating the sky, rushing directly towards him. He backed away from it and there were no more ropes on his hands or feet. He was free.

He began to run. He leapt into the air and stayed there. He was swimming through the air.

Ecstasy ran up his spine like a flickering fire, touched his back-brain, touched his mid-brain, touched his fore-brain.

EXPLOSION ALL CENTRES!

He was standing one flower among many, in a bed of tall lupins and roses which waved in a gentle wind. He pulled his roots free and began to walk.

He walked into the Lab Control Room.

Everything was normal except that gravity seemed a little heavy. Everything was as he'd left it.

He saw that he had left the Towers rotating. He went into the room he used as a bedroom and workroom. He parted the blind and looked out into the night. There was a big, full moon hanging in the deep, blue sky over the ruins of Hampton. He saw its light reflected in the faraway sea. A few bodies still lay prone near the lab. He went back into the Control Room and switched off the towers.

Returning to the bedroom he looked at the card-table he had his notes on. They were undisturbed. Neatly, side by side near a large, tattered notebook, lay a half-full ampoule of M-A 19 and a hypodermic syringe. He picked up the ampoule and threw it in a corner. It did not break but rolled around on the floor for a few seconds.

He sat down.

His whole body ached.

He picked up a sheaf of his more recent notes. He wrote everything down that came into his head on the subject of tranquilomats; it helped him think better and made sure that his drugged mind and body did not hamper him as much as they might have done if he had simply relied on his memory.

He looked at his wrists. They carried the marks of the rope. Evidently the transition from the other world to his own involved leaving anything in the other world behind. He was glad. If he hadn't, he'd have had a hell of a job getting himself untied. He shuddered—a mob might have reached the lab before he could get free and activate the Towers.

He tried hard to forget the questions flooding through his mind. Where had he been? Who were the people? What did they really want? How far could they keep a check on him? How did the M-A 19 work to aid his transport into the other world? Could they get at him here?

He decided they couldn't get at him, otherwise they might have tried earlier. Somehow it was the M-A 19 in his brain which allowed them to get hold of him. Well, that was simple—no more M-A 19.

With a feeling of relief, he forced himself to concentrate on his notes.

Out of the confusion, something seemed to be developing, but he had to work at great speed—greater speed than previously, perhaps, for he daren't use the M-A 19 again and there was nothing else left of much good.

His brain cleared as he once again got interested in his notes. He worked for two hours, making fresh notes, equations, checking his knowledge against the stack of earlier research notes by the wall near his camp bed.

Dawn was coming as he realized suddenly that he was suffering from thirst. His throat was bone dry, so was his mouth and lips. He got up and his legs felt weak. He staggered, almost knocking over the chair. With a great effort he righted it and, leaning for support on the bed, got himself to the hand-basin. It was filled by a tank near the roof and he had used it sparsely. But this time he didn't care. He stuck his head under the tap and drank the stale water greedily. It did no good. His whole body now seemed cold, his skin tight, his heart thumping heavily against his ribs. His head was aching horribly and his breathing increased.

He went and lay down on the bed, hoping the feeling would leave him.

It got worse. He needed something to cure himself.
What? he asked.
M-A 19, he answered.
NO!
But—Yes, yes, yes. All he needed was a small shot of the drug and he would be all right. He knew it.
And with knowing that, he realized something else.
He was hooked.
The drug was habit-forming.

Three

He found the half-full M-A 19 ampoule under the bed where it had rolled. He found the needle on the table where he had left it, buried under his notes. He found a vein in his forearm and shot himself full. There was no thought to Seward's action. There was just the craving and the chance of satisfying that craving.

The M-A 19 began to swim leisurely through his veins, drifting up his spine—

It hit his brain with a powerful explosion.

He was walking through a world of phosphorescent rain, leaping over large purple rocks that welcomed his feet, drew them down towards them. All was agony and startling. Now.

No-time, no-space, just the throbbing voice in the air above him. It was talking to him.

DOOM, Seward. DOOM, Seward. DOOM, Seward.

"Seward is doomed!" he laughed. "Seward is betrayed!"

Towers Advance. Towers Recede. Towers Rotate At Normal Speed.

Carnival Aktion. All Carnivals To Explode.

Up into the back-brain, into the mid-brain, on to the fore-brain.

EXPLOSION ALL CENTRES!

He was back in the torture chamber, though standing up. In the corner near the brazier the grotesque pair were muttering to one another. Mr Hand darted him an angry glance, his lips drawn over his gums in an expression of outrage.

"Hello, Seward," said the Man Without A Navel behind him. "So you're back."

"Back," said Seward heavily. "What more do you want?"

"Only your All, Seward, old man. I remember a time in Dartford before the war . . ."

"Which war?"

"Your war, Seward. You were too young to share any other. You don't remember *that* war. You weren't born. Leave it to those who *do*, Seward."

Seward turned. "My war?" He looked with disgust at the Man Without A Navel; at his reptilian blue skin and his warm-cold, dark-light, good-evil eyes. At his small yet well-formed body.

The Man Without A Navel smiled. "*Our* war, then, old man. I won't quibble."

"You made me do it. I think that somehow you made me suggest Experiment Restoration!"

"I said we won't quibble, Seward," said the man in an authoritative tone. Then, more conversationally: "I remember a time in Dartford before the war, when you sat in your arm-chair—one rather like mine—at your brother-in-law's house. Remember what you said, old man?"

Seward remembered well. "If," he quoted, "if I had a button and could press it and destroy the entire universe and myself with it, I would. For no reason other than boredom."

"Very good, Seward. You have an excellent memory."

"Is that all you're going on? Something I said out of frustration because nobody was recognizing my work?" He paused as he realized something else. "You know all about me, don't you?" he said bitterly. There seemed to be nothing he didn't know. On the other hand Seward knew nothing of the man. Nothing of this world. Nothing of where it was in space and time. It was a world of insanity, of bizarre contrasts. "*How* do you know all this?"

"Inside information, Seward, old boy."

"You're mad!"

The Man Without A Navel returned to his earlier topic. "Are you bored now, Seward?"

"Bored? No. Tired, yes."

"Bored, no—tired, yes. Very good, Seward. You got here later than expected. What kept you?" The man laughed.

"I kept me. I held off taking the M-A 19 for as long as I could."

"But you came to us in the end, eh? Good man, Seward."

"You knew the M-A 19 was habit-forming? You knew I'd have to take it, come back here?"

"Naturally."

He said pleadingly: "Let me go for God's sake! You've made me. Made me . . ."

"Your dearest wish almost come true, Seward. Isn't that what you wanted? I made you come close to destroying the world? Is that it?"

"So you *did* somehow influence Experiment Restoration!"

"It's possible. But you haven't done very well either way. The world is in shambles. You can't reverse that. Kill it off. Let's start fresh, Seward. Forget your experiments with the tranquilomats and help us."

"No."

The Man Without A Navel shrugged. "We'll see, old boy."

He looked at the mumbling men in the corner. "Morl—Hand—take Professor Seward to his room. I don't want any mistakes this time. I'm going to take him out of your hands. Obviously we need subtler minds put on the problem."

The pair came forward and grabbed Seward. The Man Without A Navel opened the door and they went through it first, forcing Seward ahead of them.

He was too demoralized to resist much, this time. Demoralized by the fact that he was hooked on M-A 19. What did the junkies call it? The Habit. He had The Habit. Demoralized by his inability to understand the whereabouts or nature of the world he was on. Demoralized by the fact that the Man Without A Navel seemed to know everything about his personal life on Earth. Demoralized that he had fallen into the man's trap. Who had developed M-A 19? He couldn't remember. Perhaps the Man Without A Navel had planted it? He supposed it might be possible.

He was pushed along another series of corridors, arrived at another door. The Man Without A Navel came up behind them and unlocked the door.

Seward was shoved into the room. It was narrow and low—coffin-like.

"We'll be sending someone along to see you in a little while, Seward," said the man lightly. The door was slammed.

Seward lay in pitch blackness.

He began to sob.

Later, he heard a noise outside. A stealthy noise of creeping feet. He shuddered. What was the torture going to be this time?

He heard a scraping and a muffled rattle. The door opened.

Against the light from the passage, Seward saw the man clearly. He was a big, fat negro in a grey suit. He wore a flowing, rainbow-coloured tie. He was grinning.

Seward liked the man instinctively. But he no longer trusted his instinct. "What do you want?" he said suspiciously.

The huge negro raised his finger to his lips. "Ssshh," he whispered. "I'm going to try to get you out of here."

"An old Secret Police trick on my world," said Seward. "I'm not falling for that."

"It's no trick, son. Even if it is, what can you lose?"

"Nothing." Seward got up.

The big man put his arm around Seward's shoulders. Seward felt comfortable in the grip, though normally he disliked such gestures.

"Now, son, we go real quietly and we go as fast as we can. Come on."

Softly, the big man began to tiptoe along the corridor. Seward was sure that TV cameras, or whatever they were, were following him, that the Man Without A Navel, the monk, the two torturers, the Laughing Cavalier, were all waiting somewhere to seize him.

But, very quickly, the negro had reached a small wooden door and was drawing a bolt. He patted Seward's shoulder and held the door open for him. "Through you go, son. Make for the red car."

It was morning. In the sky hung a golden sun, twice the size of Earth's. There was a vast expanse of lifeless rock in all directions, broken only by a white road which stretched into the distance. On the road, close to Seward, was parked a car something like a Cadillac. It was fire-red and bore the registration plates Y O U OOO. Whoever these people were, Seward decided, they were originally from Earth—all except the Man Without A Navel, perhaps. Possibly this was his world and the others had been brought from Earth, like him.

He walked towards the car. The air was cold and fresh. He stood by the convertible and looked back. The negro was running over the rock towards him. He dashed round the car and got into the driver's seat. Seward got in beside him.

The negro started the car, put it into gear and shoved his foot down hard on the accelerator pedal. The car jerked away and had reached top speed in seconds.

At the wheel, the negro relaxed. "Glad that went smoothly. I didn't expect to get away with it so easily, son. You're Seward, aren't you?"

"Yes. You seem to be as well-informed as the others."

"I guess so." The negro took a pack of cigarettes from his shirt pocket. "Smoke?"

"No thanks," said Seward. "That's one habit I don't have."

The negro looked back over his shoulder. The expanse of rock seemed never-ending, though in the distance the fortress was disappearing. He flipped a cigarette out of the pack and put it between his lips. He unclipped the car's lighter and put it to the tip of his cigarette. He inhaled and put the lighter back. The cigarette between his lips, he returned his other hand to the wheel.

He said: "They were going to send the Vampire to you. It's lucky I reached you in time."

"It could be," said Seward. "Who are you? What part do you play in this?"

"Let's just say I'm a friend of yours and an enemy of your enemies. The name's Farlowe."

"Well, I trust you, Farlowe—though God knows why."

Farlowe grinned. "Why not? I don't want your world destroyed any more than you do. It doesn't much matter, I guess, but if there's a chance of restoring it, then you ought to try."

"Then you're from my world originally, is that it?"

"In a manner of speaking, son," said Farlowe.

Very much later, the rock gave way to pleasant, flat countryside with trees, fields and little cottages peaceful under the vast sky. In the distance, Seward saw herds of cattle and sheep, the occasional horse. It reminded him of the countryside of his childhood, all clear and fresh and sharp with the clarity that only a child's eye can bring to a scene before it is obscured and tainted by the impressions of adulthood. Soon the flat country was behind them and they were going through an area of low, green hills, the huge sun flooding the scene with its soft, golden light. There were no clouds in the pale blue sky.

The big car sped smoothly along and Seward, in the comfortable companionship of Farlowe, began to relax a little. He felt almost happy, would have felt happy if it had not been for the nagging knowledge that somehow he had to get back and continue his work. It was not merely a question of restoring sanity to the world, now—he had also to thwart whatever plans were in the mind of The Man Without A Navel.

After a long silence, Seward asked a direct question. "Farlowe, where is this world? What are we doing here?"

Farlowe's answer was vague. He stared ahead at the road. "Don't ask me that, son. I don't rightly know."

"But you live here."

"So do you."

"No—I only come here when—when . . ."

"When what?"

But Seward couldn't raise the courage to admit about the drug to Farlowe. Instead he said: "Does M-A 19 mean anything to you?"

"Nope."

So Farlowe hadn't come here because of the drug. Seward said: "But you said you were from my world originally."

"Only in a manner of speaking." Farlowe changed gears as the road curved steeply up a hill. It rose gently above the idyllic countryside below.

Seward changed his line of questioning. "Isn't there any sort of organization here—no government. What's the name of this country?"

Farlowe shrugged. "It's just a place—no government. The people in the fortress run most things. Everybody's scared of them."

"I don't blame them. Who's the Vampire you mentioned?"

"He works for the Man."

"What is he?"

"Why—a vampire, naturally," said Farlowe in surprise.

The sun had started to set and the whole countryside was bathed in red-gold light. The car continued to climb the long hill.

Farlowe said: "I'm taking you to some friends. You ought to be fairly safe there. Then maybe we can work out a way of getting you back."

Seward felt better. At least Farlowe had given him some direct information.

As the car reached the top of the hill and began to descend Seward got a view of an odd and disturbing sight. The sun was like a flat, round, red disc—yet only half of it was above the horizon. *The line of the horizon evenly intersected the sun's disc!* It was some sort of mirage—yet so convincing that Seward looked away, staring instead at the black smoke which he could now see rolling across the valley below. He said nothing to Farlowe.

"How much further?" he asked later as the car came to the bottom of the hill. Black night had come, moonless, and the car's headlights blazed.

"A long way yet, I'm afraid, son," said Farlowe. "You cold?"

"No."

"We'll be hitting a few signs of civilization soon. You tired?"

"No—why?"

"We could put up at a motel or something. I guess we could eat anyway."

Ahead, Seward saw a few lights. He couldn't make out where they came from. Farlowe began to slow down. "We'll risk it," he said. He pulled in towards the lights and Seward saw that it was a line of fuel pumps. Behind the pumps was a single storey building, very long and built entirely of timber by the look of it. Farlowe drove in between the pumps and the building. A man in overalls, the top half of his face shadowed by the peak of his cap, came into sight. Farlowe got out of the car with a signal to Seward to do the same. The negro handed his keys to the attendant. "Fill her full and give her a quick check."

Could this be Earth, Seward wondered. Earth in the future—or possibly an Earth of a different space-time continuum. That was the likeliest explanation for this unlikely world. The contrast between recognizable, everyday things and the grotesqueries of the fortress was strange—yet it could be explained easily if these people had contact with his world. That would explain how they had things like cars and fuel stations and no apparent organization necessary for producing them. Somehow, perhaps, they just—*stole* them?

*   *   *

He followed Farlowe into the long building. He could see through the wide windows that it was some kind of restaurant. There was a long, clean counter and a few people seated at tables at the far end. All had their backs to him.

He and Farlowe sat down on stools. Close to them was the largest pin-table Seward had ever seen. Its lights were flashing and its balls were clattering, though there was no one operating it. The coloured lights flashed series of numbers at him until his eyes lost focus and he had to turn away.

A woman was standing behind the counter now. Most of her face was covered by a yashmak.

"What do you want to eat, son?" said Farlowe, turning to him.

"Oh, anything."

Farlowe ordered sandwiches and coffee. When the woman had gone to get their order, Seward whispered: "Why's she wearing that thing?"

Farlowe pointed at a sign Seward hadn't noticed before. It read THE HAREM HAVEN. "It's their gimmick," said Farlowe.

Seward looked back at the pin-table. The lights had stopped flashing, the balls had stopped clattering. But above it suddenly appeared a huge pair of disembodied eyes. He gasped.

Distantly, he heard his name being repeated over and over again. "Seward. Seward. Seward. Seward . . ."

He couldn't tell where the voice was coming from. He glanced up at the ceiling. Not from there. The voice stopped. He looked back at the pin-table. They dyes had vanished. His panic returned. He got off his stool.

"I'll wait for you in the car, Farlowe."

Farlowe looked surprised. "What's the matter, son?"

"Nothing—it's okay—I'll wait in the car."

Farlowe shrugged.

Seward went out into the night. The attendant had gone but the car was waiting for him. He opened the door and climbed in.

What did the eyes mean? Were the people from the fortress following him in some way. Suddenly an explanation for most of the questions bothering him sprang into his mind. Of course—telepathy. They were probably telepaths. That was how they knew so much about him. That could be how they knew of his world and could influence events there—

they might never go there in person. This comforted him a little, though he realized that getting out of this situation was going to be even more difficult than he'd thought.

He looked through the windows and saw Farlowe's big body perched on its stool. The other people in the cafe were still sitting with their backs to him. He realized that there was something familiar about them.

He saw Farlowe get up and walk towards the door. He came out and got into the car, slamming the door after him. He leaned back in his seat and handed Seward a sandwich. "You seem worked up, son," he said. "You'd better eat this."

Seward took the sandwich. He was staring at the backs of the other customers again. He frowned.

Farlowe started the car and they moved towards the road. Then Seward realized who the men reminded him of. He craned his head back in the hope of seeing their faces, but it was too late. They had reminded him of his dead assistants—the men who'd committed suicide.

They roared through dimly-seen towns—all towers and angles. There seemed to be nobody about. Dawn came up and they still sped on. Seward realized that Farlowe must have a tremendous vitality, for he didn't seem to tire at all. Also, perhaps, he was motivated by a desire to get as far away from the fortress as possible.

They stopped twice to re-fuel and Farlowe bought more sandwiches and coffee which they had as they drove.

In the late afternoon Farlowe said: "Almost there."

They passed through a pleasant village. It was somehow alien, although very similar to a small English village. It had an oddly foreign look which was hard to place. Farlowe pulled in at what seemed to be the gates of a large public park. He looked up at the sun. "Just made it," he said. "Wait in the park—someone will come to collect you."

"You're leaving me?"

"Yes. I don't think they know where you are. They'll look but, with luck, they won't look around here. Out you get, son. Into the park."

"Who do I wait for?"

"You'll know her when she comes."

"Her?" He got out and closed the door. He stood on the pavement watching as, with a cheerful wave, Farlowe drove off. He felt a tremendous sense of loss then, as if his only hope had been taken away.

Gloomily, he turned and walked through the park gates.

Four

As he walked between low hedges along a gravel path, he realized that this park, like so many things in this world, contrasted with the village it served. It was completely familiar just like a park on his own world.

It was like a grey, hazy winter's afternoon, with the brittle, interwoven skeletons of trees black and sharp against the cold sky. Birds perched on trees and bushes, or flew noisily into the silent air.

Evergreens crowded upon the leaf-strewn grass. Cry of sparrows. Peacocks, necks craned forward, dived towards scattered bread. Silver birch, larch, elm, monkey-puzzle trees, and swaying white ferns, each one like an ostrich feather stuck in the earth. A huge, ancient, nameless trunk from which, at the top, grew an expanse of soft, yellow fungus; the trunk itself looking like a Gothic cliff, full of caves and dark windows. A grey and brown pigeon perched motionless on the slender branches of a young birch. Peacock chicks the size of hens pecked with concentration at the grass.

Mellow, nostalgic smell of winter; distant sounds of children playing; lost black dog looking for master; red disc of sun in the cool, darkening sky. The light was sharp and yet soft, peaceful. A path led into the distance towards a flight of wide stone steps, at the top of which was the curving entrance to an arbour, browns, blacks, and yellows of sapless branches and fading leaves.

From the arbour a girl appeared and began to descend the steps with quick, graceful movements. She stopped when she reached the path. She looked at him. She had long, blonde hair and wore a white dress with a full skirt. She was about seventeen.

The peace of the park was suddenly interrupted by children rushing from nowhere towards the peacocks, laughing and shouting. Some of the boys saw the tree trunk and made for it. Others stood looking upwards at the sun as it sank in the cold air. They seemed not to see either Seward or the girl. Seward looked at her. Did he recognize her? It wasn't possible. Yet she, too, gave him a look of recognition, smiled shyly at him and ran towards him. She reached him, stood on tiptoe and gave him a light kiss on the cheek.

"Hello, Lee."

"Hello. Have you come to find me?"

"I've been looking for you a long time."

"Farlowe sent a message ahead?"

She took his hand. "Come on. Where have you been, Lee?"

This was a question he couldn't answer. He let her lead him back up the steps, through the arbour. Between the branches he glanced a garden and a pool. "Come on," she said. "Let's see what's for dinner. Mother's looking forward to meeting you."

He no longer questioned how these strange people all seemed to know his name. It was still possible that all of them were taking part in the conspiracy against him.

At the end of the arbour was a house, several storeys high. It was a pleasant house with a blue and white door. She led him up the path and into a hallway. It was shining with dark polished wood and brass plates on the walls. From a room at the end he smelled spicy cooking. She went first and opened the door at the end. "Mother—Lee Seward's here. Can we come in?"

"Of course." The voice was warm, husky, full of humour. They went into the room and Seward saw a woman of about forty, very well preserved, tall, large-boned with a fine-featured face and smiling mouth. Her eyes also smiled. Her sleeves were rolled up and she put the lid back on a pan on the stove.

"How do you do, Professor Seward. Mr Farlowe's told us about you. You're in trouble, I hear."

"How do you do, Mrs—"

"Call me Martha. Has Sally introduced herself?"

"No," Sally laughed. "I forgot. I'm Sally, Lee."

Her mother gave a mock frown. "I suppose you've been calling our guest by his first name, as usual. Do you mind, professor?"

"Not at all." He was thinking how attractive they both were, in their different ways. The young, fresh girl and her warm, intelligent mother. He had always enjoyed the company of women, but never so much, he realized, as now. They seemed to complement one another. In their presence he felt safe, at ease. Now he realized why Farlowe had chosen them to hide him. Whatever the facts, he would *feel* safe here.

Martha was saying: "Dinner won't be long."

"It smells good."

"Probably smells better than it tastes," she laughed. "Go into the lounge with Sally. Sally, fix Professor Seward a drink."

"Call me Lee," said Seward, a little uncomfortably. He had never cared much for his first name. He preferred his middle name, William, but not many others did.

"Come on, Lee," she took his hand and led him out of the kitchen. "We'll see what there is." They went into a small, well-lighted lounge. The furniture, like the whole house, had a look that was half-familiar, half-alien—obviously the product of a slightly different race. Perhaps they deliberately imitated Earth culture, without quite succeeding. Sally still gripped his hand. Her hand was warm and her skin smooth. He made to drop it but, involuntarily, squeezed it gently before she took it away to deal with the drink. She gave him another shy smile. He felt that she was as attracted to him as he was to her. "What's it going to be?" she asked him.

"Oh, anything," he said, sitting down on a comfortable sofa. She poured him a dry martini and brought it over. Then she sat demurely down beside him and watched him drink it. Her eyes sparkled with a mixture of sauciness and innocence which he found extremely appealing. He looked around the room.

"How did Farlowe get his message to you?" he said.

"He came the other day. Said he was going to try and get into the fortress and help you. Farlowe's always flitting about. I think the people at the fortress have a price on his head or something. It's exciting, isn't it."

"You can say that again," Seward said feelingly.

"Why are they after you?"

"They want me to help them destroy the world I come from. Do you know anything about it?"

"Earth, isn't it?"

"Yes." Was he going to get some straightforward answers at last?

"I know it's very closely connected with ours and that some of us want to escape from here and go to your world."

"Why?" he asked eagerly.

She shook her head. Her long, fine hair waved with the motion. "I don't really know. Something about their being trapped here—something like that. Farlowe said something about you being a 'key' to their release. They can only do what they want to do with your agreement."

"But I could agree and then break my word!"

"I don't think you could—but honestly, I don't know any more. I've probably got it wrong. Do you like me, Lee?"

He was startled by the directness of her question. "Yes," he said, "very much."

"Farlowe said you would. Good, isn't it?"

"Why—yes. Farlowe knows a lot."

"That's why he works against *them*."

Martha came in. "Almost ready," she smiled. "I think I'll have a quick one before I start serving. How are you feeling Lee, after your ride?"

"Fine," he said, "fine." He had never been in a position like this one—with two women either of whom was extremely attractive for almost opposite reasons.

"We were discussing why the people at the fortress wanted my help," he said, turning the conversation back the way he felt it ought to go if he was ever going to get off this world and back to his own and his work.

"Farlowe said something about it."

"Yes, Sally told me. Does Farlowe belong to some sort of underground organization?"

"Underground? Why, yes, in a way he does."

"Aren't they strong enough to fight the Man Without A Navel and his friends?"

"Farlowe says they're strong enough, but divided over what should be done and how."

"I see. That's fairly common amongst such groups, I believe."

"Yes."

"What part do you play?"

"None, really. Farlowe asked me to put you up—that's all." She sipped her drink, her eyes smiling directly into his. He drained his glass.

"Shall we eat?" she said. "Sally, take Lee in to the dining-room."

The girl got up and, somewhat possessively Seward thought, linked her arm in his. Her young body against his was distracting. He felt a little warm. She took him in. The

Michael Moorcock

table was laid for supper. Three chairs and three places. The sun had set and candles burned on the table in brass candelabras. She unlinked her arm and pulled out one of the chairs.

"You sit here, Lee—at the head of the table." She grinned. Then she leaned forward as he sat down. "Hope mummy isn't boring you."

He was surprised. "Why should she?"

Martha came in with three covered dishes on a tray. "This may not have turned out quite right, Lee. Never does when you're trying hard."

"I'm sure it'll be fine," he smiled. The two women sat down on either side of him. Martha served him. It was some sort of goulash with vegetables. He took his napkin and put it on his lap.

As they began to eat, Martha said: "How is it?"

"Fine," he said. It was very good. Apart from the feeling that some kind of rivalry for his attentions existed between mother and daughter the air of normality in the house was comforting. Here, he might be able to do some constructive thinking about his predicament.

When the meal was over, Martha said: "It's time for bed, Sally. Say good night to Lee."

She pouted. "Oh, it's not fair."

"Yes it is," she said firmly. "You can see Lee in the morning. He's had a long journey."

"All right." She smiled at Seward. "Sleep well, Lee."

"I think I will," he said.

Martha chuckled after Sally had gone. "Would you like a drink before you go to bed?" She spoke softly.

"Love one," he said.

They went into the other room. He sat down on the sofa as she mixed the drinks. She brought them over and sat down next to him as her daughter had done earlier.

"Tell me everything that's been happening. It sounds so exciting."

He knew at once he could tell her all he wanted to, that she would listen and be sympathetic. "It's terrifying, really," he began, half-apologetically. He began to talk, beginning with what had happened on Earth. She listened.

"I even wondered if this was a dream-world—a figment of my imagination," he finished, "but I had to reject that when I went back to my own. I had rope marks on my wrists—my hair was soaking wet. You don't get that in a dream!"

"I hope not," she smiled. "We're different here, Lee, obviously. Our life doesn't have the—the *shape* that yours has. We haven't much direction, no real desires. We just—well—*exist*. It's as if we're waiting for something to happen. As if—" she paused and seemed to be looking down deep into herself. "Put it this way—Farlowe thinks you're the key figure in some development that's happening here. Supposing—supposing we were some kind of—of experiment . . ."

"Experiment? How do you mean?"

"Well, from what you say, the people at the fortress have an advanced science that we don't know about. Supposing our parents, say, had been kidnapped from your world and—made to think—what's the word—"

"Conditioned?"

"Yes, conditioned to think they were natives of this world. We'd have grown up knowing nothing different. Maybe the Man Without A Navel is a member of an alien race—a scientist of some kind in charge of the experiment."

"But why should they make such a complicated experiment?"

"So they could study us, I suppose."

Seward marvelled at her deductive powers. She had come to a much firmer theory than he had. But then he thought, she might subconsciously *know* the truth. Everyone knew much more than they knew, as it were. For instance, it was pretty certain that the secret of the tranquilomat was locked somewhere down in his unconscious if only he could get at it. Her explanation was logical and worth thinking about.

"You may be right," he said. "If so, it's something to go on. But it doesn't stop my reliance on the drug—or the fact that the Man and his helpers are probably telepathic and are at this moment looking for me."

She nodded. "Could there be an *antidote* for the drug?"

"Unlikely. Drugs like that don't really need antidotes—they're not like poisons. There must be some way of getting at the people in the fortress—some way of putting a stop to their plans. What about an organized revolution? What has Farlowe tried to do?"

"Nothing much. The people aren't easy to organize. We haven't much to do with one another. Farlowe was probably hoping you could help—think of something he hasn't. Maybe one of those machines you mentioned would work against the fortress people?"

"No, I don't think so. Anyway, the hallucinomats are too big to move from one place to another by hand—let alone from one world to another."

"And you haven't been able to build a tranquilomat yet?"

"No—we have a lot of experimental machines lying around at the lab—they're fairly small—but it's a question of modifying them—that's what I'm trying to do at the moment. If I could make one that works it would solve part of my problem—it would save my world and perhaps even save yours, if you *are* in a state of conditioning."

"It sounds reasonable," she dropped her eyes and looked at her drink. She held the glass balanced on her knees which were pressed closely together, nearly touching him. "But," she said, "they're going to catch you sooner or later. They're very powerful. They're sure to catch you. Then they'll make you agree to their idea."

"Why are you so certain?"

"I know them."

He let that go. She said: "Another drink?" and got up.

"Yes, please." He got up, too, and extended his glass, then went closer to her. She put bottle and glass on the table and looked into his face. There was compassion, mystery, tenderness in her large, dark eyes. He smelled her perfume, warm, pleasant. He put his arms around her and kissed her. "My room," she said. They went upstairs.

Later that night, feeling strangely revitalized, he left the bed and the sleeping Martha and went and stood beside the window overlooking the silent park. He felt cold and he picked up his shirt and trousers, put them on. He sighed. He felt his mind clear and his body relax. He must work out a way of travelling from this world to his own at will—that might put a stop to the plans of the Man Without A Navel.

He turned guiltily as he heard the door open. Sally was standing there. She wore a long, white, flowing nightdress.

"Lee! I came to tell mummy—what are you doing in here?" Her eyes were horrified, accusing him. Martha sat up suddenly.

"Sally—what's the matter!"

Lee stepped forward. "Listen, Sally. Don't—"

Sally shrugged, but tears had come to her eyes. "I thought you wanted *me*! Now I know—I shouldn't have brought you here. Farlowe said—"

"What did Farlowe say?"

"He said you'd want to marry me!"

"But that's ridiculous. How could he say that? I'm a stranger here. You were to hide me from the fortress people, that's all."

But she had only picked up one word. "Ridiculous. Yes, I suppose it is, when my own mother . . ."

"Sally—you'd better go to bed. We'll discuss it in the morning," said Martha softly. "What was it you came in about?"

Sally laughed theatrically. "It doesn't matter now." She slammed the door.

Seward looked at Martha. "I'm sorry, Martha."

"It wasn't your fault—or mine. Sally's romantic and young."

"And jealous," Seward sat down on the bed. The feeling of comfort, of companionship, of bringing some order out of chaos—it had all faded. "Look, Martha, I can't stay here."

"You're running away?"

"If you like—but—well—the two of you—I'm in the middle."

"I guessed that. No, you'd better stay. We'll work something out."

"Okay." He got up, sighing heavily. "I think I'll go for a walk in the park—it may help me to think. I'd just reached the stage where I was getting somehwere. Thanks for that, anyway, Martha."

She smiled. "Don't worry, Lee. I'll have everything running smoothly again by tomorrow."

He didn't doubt it. She was a remarkable woman.

He put on his socks and shoes, opened the door and went out on to the landing. Moonlight entered through a tall, slender window at the end. He went down the two flights of stairs and out of the front door. He turned into the lane and entered the arbour. In the cool of the night, he once again was able to begin some constructive thinking.

While he was on this world, he would not waste his time, he would keep trying to discover the necessary modifications to make the tranquilomats workable.

He wandered through the arbour, keeping any thoughts of the two women out of his mind. He turned into another section of the arbour he hadn't noticed before. The turnings became numerous but he was scarcely aware of them. It was probably some sort of child's maze.

He paused as he came to a bench. He sat down and folded his arms in front of him, concentrating on his problem.

Much later he heard a sound to his right and looked up.

A man he didn't know was standing there, grinning at him.

Seward noticed at once that the man had overlong canines, that he smelt of damp earth and decay. He wore a black, polo-neck pullover and black, stained trousers. His face was waxen and very pale.

"I've been looking for you for ages, Professor Seward," said the Vampire.

Five

Seward got up and faced the horrible creature. The Vampire continued to smile. He didn't move. Seward felt revulsion.

"It's been a long journey," said the Vampire in a sibilant voice like the sound of a frigid wind blowing through dead boughs. "I had intended to visit you at the fortress, but when I got to your room you had left. I was disappointed."

"Doubtless," said Seward. "Well, you've had a wasted journey. I'm not going back there until I'm ready."

"That doesn't interest me."

"What does?" Seward tried to stop himself from trembling.

The Vampire put his hands into his pockets. "Only you."

"Get away from here. You're outnumbered—I have friends." But he knew that his tone was completely unconvincing.

The Vampire hissed his amusement. "They can't do much, Seward."

"What are you—some sort of android made to frighten people?"

"No." The Vampire took a pace forward.

Suddenly he stopped as a voice came faintly from somewhere in the maze.

"Lee! Lee! Where are you?"

It was Sally's voice.

"Stay away, Sally!" Lee called.

"But I was going to warn you. I saw the Vampire from the window. He's somewhere in the park."

"I know. Go home!"

"I'm sorry about the scene, Lee. I wanted to apologize. It was childish."

"It doesn't matter." He looked at the Vampire. He was standing in a relaxed position, hands in pockets, smiling. "Go home, Sally!"

"She won't, you know," whispered the Vampire.

Her voice was closer. "Lee, I must talk to you."

He screamed: "Sally—the Vampire's here. Go home. Warn your mother, not me. Get some help if you can—but go home!"

Now he saw her enter the part of the maze he was in. She gasped as she saw them. He was between her and the Vampire.

"Sally—do what I told you."

But the Vampire's cold eyes widened and he took one hand out of his pocket and crooked a finger. "Come here, Sally."

She began to walk forward.

He turned to the Vampire. "What do you want?"

"Only a little blood—yours, perhaps—or the young lady's."

"Damn you. Get away. Go back, Sally." She didn't seem to hear him.

He daren't touch the cold body, the earth-damp clothes. He stepped directly between the girl and the Vampire.

He felt sick, but he reached out his hands and shoved at the creature's body. Flesh yielded, but bone did not. The Vampire held his ground, smiling, staring beyond Seward at the girl.

Seward shoved again and suddenly the creature's arms clamped around him and the grinning, fanged face darted towards his. The thing's breath disgusted him. He struggled, but could not break the Vampire's grasp.

A cold mouth touched his neck. He yelled and kicked. He felt a tiny pricking against his throat. Sally screamed. He heard her turn and run and felt a fraction of relief.

He punched with both fists as hard as he could into the creature's solar plexus. It worked. The Vampire groaned and let go. Seward was disgusted to see that its fangs dripped with blood.

His blood.

Now rage helped him. He chopped at the Vampire's throat. It gasped, tottered, and fell in a sprawl of loose limbs to the ground.

Panting, Seward kicked it in the head. It didn't move.

He bent down and rolled the Vampire over. As far as he could tell it was dead. He tried to remember what he'd read about legendary vampires. Not much. Something about a stake through its heart. Well, that was out.

But the thought that struck him most was that he had fought one of the fortress people—and had won. It was possible to beat them!

He walked purposefully through the maze. It wasn't as tortuous as he'd supposed. Soon he emerged at the arbour entrance near the house. He saw Sally and Martha running towards him. Behind them, another figure lumbered. Farlowe. He had got here fast.

"Seward," he shouted. "They said the Vampire had got you!"

"I got him," said Seward as they came up and stopped.

"What?"

"I beat him."

"But—that's impossible."

Seward shrugged. He felt elated. "Evidently, it's possible," he said. "I knocked him out. He seems to be dead—but I suppose you never know with vampires."

Farlowe was astonished. "I believe you," he said, "but it's fantastic. How did you do it?"

"I got frightened and then angry," said Seward simply. "Maybe you've been over-awed by these people too long."

"It seems like it," Farlowe admitted. "Let's go and have a look at him. Sally and Martha had better stay behind."

Seward led him back through the maze. The Vampire was still where he'd fallen. Farlowe touched the corpse with his foot.

"That's the Vampire all right." He grinned. "I knew we had a winner in you, son. What are you going to do now?"

"I'm going straight back to the fortress and get this worked out once and for all. Martha gave me an idea yesterday evening and she may well be right. I'm going to try and find out anyway."

"Better not be over-confident, son."

"Better than being over-cautious."

"Maybe," Farlowe agreed doubtfully. "What's this idea Martha gave you?"

"It's really her idea, complete. Let her explain. She's an intelligent woman—and she's bothered to think about this problem from scratch. I'd advise you to do the same."

"I'll hear what it is, first. Let's deal with the Vampire and then get back to the house."

"I'll leave the Vampire to you. I want to use your car."

"Why?"

"To go back to the fortress."

"Don't be a fool. Wait until we've got some help."

"I can't wait that long, Farlowe. I've got other work to do back on my own world."

"Okay," Farlowe shrugged.

Farlowe faded.

The maze began to fade.

Explosions in the brain.

Vertigo.

Sickness.

His head ached and he could not breathe. He yelled, but he had no voice. Multicoloured explosions in front of his eyes. He was whirling round and round, spinning rapidly. Then he felt a new surface dragging at his feet. He closed his eyes and stumbled against something. He fell on to something soft.

It was his camp bed. He was back in his laboratory.

Seward wasted no time wondering what had happened. He knew more or less. Possibly his encounter with the Vampire had sent him back—the exertion or—of course—the creature had drawn some of his blood. Maybe that was it. He felt the pricking sensation, still. He went to the mirror near the wash-stand. He could just see the little marks in his neck. Further proof that wherever that world was it was as real as the one he was in now.

He went to the table and picked up his notes, then walked into the other room. In one section was a long bench. On it, in various stages of dismantling, were the machines that he had been working on, the tranquilomats that somehow just didn't work. He picked up one of the smallest and checked its batteries, its lenses and its sonic agitator. The idea with this one was to use a combination of light and sound to agitate certain dormant cells in the brain. Long since, psychophysicists had realized that mental abnormality had a chemical as well as a mental cause. Just as a patient with a psychosomatic illness produced all the biological symptoms, of whatever disease he thought he had, so did chemistry play a part in brain disorders. Whether the change in the brain cells came first or afterwards they weren't sure. But the fact was that the cells could be agitated and the mind, by a mixture of hypnosis and conditioning, could be made to work normally. But it was a long step from knowing this and being able to use the information in the construction of tranquilomats.

Seward began to work on the machine. He felt he was on the right track, at least.

But how long could he keep going before his need for the drug destroyed his will?

He kept going some five hours before his withdrawal symptoms got the better of him.

He staggered towards one of the drug-drawers and fumbled out an ampoule of M-A 19. He staggered into his bedroom and reached for the needle on the table.

He filled the syringe. He filled his veins. He filled his brain with a series of explosions which blew him clean out of his own world into the other.

Fire flew up his spine. Ignited back-brain, ignited mid-brain, ignited fore-brain. Ignited all centres.

EXPLOSION ALL CENTRES.

This time the transition was brief. He was standing in the part of the maze where he'd been when he'd left. The Vampire's corpse was gone. Farlowe had gone, also. He experienced a feeling of acute frustration that he couldn't continue with his work on KLTM-8—the tranquilomat he'd been modifying when his craving for the M-A 19 took over.

But there was something to do here, too.

He left the maze and walked towards the house. It was dawn and very cold. Farlowe's car was parked there. He noticed the licence number. It seemed different. It now said YOU 009. Maybe he'd mistaken the last digit for a zero last time he'd looked.

The door was ajar. Farlowe and Martha were standing in the hall.

They looked surprised when he walked in.

"I thought the Vampire was peculiar, son," said Farlowe. "But yours was the best vanishing act I've ever seen."

"Martha will explain that, too," Seward said, not looking at her. "Has she told you her theory?"

"Yes, it sounds feasible." He spoke slowly, looking at the floor. He looked up. "We got rid of the Vampire. Burned him up. He burns well."

"That's one out of the way, at least," said Seward. "How many others are there at the fortress?"

Farlowe shook his head. "Not sure. How many did you see?"

"The Man Without A Navel, a character called Brother Sebastian who wears a cowl and probably isn't human either, two pleasant gentlemen called Mr Morl and Mr Hand—and a man in fancy dress whose name I don't know."

"There are one or two more," Farlowe said. "But it's not their numbers we've got to worry about—it's their power!"

"I think maybe it's over-rated," Seward said.

"You may be right, son."

"I'm going to find out."

"You still want my car?"

"Yes. If you want to follow up behind with whatever help you can gather, do that."

"I will," Farlowe glanced at Martha. "What do you think, Martha?"

"I think he may succeed," she said. "Good luck, Lee." She smiled at him in a way that made him want to stay.

"Right," said Seward. "I'm going. Hope to see you there."

"I may be wrong, Lee," she said warningly. "It was only an idea."

"It's the best one I've heard. Goodbye."

He went out of the house and climbed into the car.

Six

The road was white, the sky was blue, the car was red and the countryside was green. Yet there was less clarity about the scenery than Seward remembered. Perhaps it was because he no longer had the relaxing company of Farlowe, because his mind was working furiously and his emotions at full blast.

Whoever had designed the set-up on this world had done it well, but had missed certain details. Seward realized that one of the "alien" aspects of the world was that everything was just a little too new. Even Farlowe's car looked as if it had just been driven off the production line.

By the early afternoon he was beginning to feel tired and some of his original impetus had flagged. He decided to move in to the side of the road and rest for a short time, stretch his legs. He stopped the car and got out.

He walked over to the other side of the road. It was on a hillside and he could look down over a wide, shallow valley. A river gleamed in the distance, there were cottages and livestock in the fields. He couldn't see the horizon. Far away he saw a great bank of reddish-looking clouds that seemed to swirl and seethe like a restless ocean. For all the *signs* of habitation, the countryside had taken on a desolate quality as if it had been abandoned. He could not believe that there were people living in the cottages and tending the livestock. The whole thing looked like the set for a film. Or a play—a complicated play devised by the Man Without A Navel and his friends—a play in which the fate of a world—possibly two worlds—was at stake.

How soon would the play resolve itself? he wondered, as he turned back towards the car.

A woman was standing by the car. She must have come down the hill while he was looking at the valley. She had long, jet black hair and big, dark eyes. Her skin was tanned dark gold. She had full, extraordinarily sensuous lips. She wore a well-tailored red suit, a black blouse, black shoes and black handbag. She looked rather sheepish. She raised her head to look at him and as she did so a lock of her black hair fell over her eyes. She brushed it back.

"Hello," she said. "Am I lucky!"

"Are you?"

"I hope so. I didn't expect to find a car on the road. You haven't broken down have you?" She asked this last question anxiously.

"No," he said. "I stopped for a rest. How did you get here?"

She pointed up the hill. "There's a little track up there—a cattle-track, I suppose. My car skidded and went into a tree. It's a wreck."

"I'll have a look at it for you."

She shook her head. "There's no point—it's a write-off. Can you give me a lift?"

"Where are you going?" he said unwillingly.

"Well, it's about sixty miles that way," she pointed in the direction he was going. "A small town."

It wouldn't take long to drive sixty miles on a road as clear as this with no apparent speed-limit. He scratched his head doubtfully. The woman was a diversion he hadn't expected and, in a way, resented. But she was very attractive. He couldn't refuse her. He hadn't seen any car-tracks leading off the road. This, as far as he knew, was the only one, but it was possible he hadn't noticed since he didn't know this world. Also, he decided, the woman evidently wasn't involved in the struggle between the fortress people and Farlowe's friends. She was probably just one of the conditioned, living out her life completely unaware of where she was and why. He might be able to get some information out of her.

"Get in," he said.

"Oh, thanks." She got in, seeming rather deliberately to show him a lot of leg. He opened his door and slid under the wheel. She sat uncomfortably close to him. He started the engine and moved the car out on to the road again.

"I'm a stranger here," he began conversationally. "What about you?"

"Not me—I've lived hereabouts all my life. Where do you come from—stranger?"

He smiled. "A long way away."

"Are they all as good looking as you?" It was trite, but it worked. He felt flattered.

"Not any more," he said. That was true. Maniacs never looked very good. But this wasn't the way he wanted the conversation to go, however nice the direction. He said: "You're not very heavily populated around here. I haven't seen another car, or another person for that matter, since I set off this morning."

"It does get boring," she said. She smiled at him. That and her full body, her musky scent and her closeness, made him breathe more heavily than he would have liked. One thing about this world—the women were considerably less inhibited than on his own. It was a difference in population, perhaps. In an overcrowded world your social behaviour must be more rigid, out of necessity.

He kept his hands firmly on the wheel and his eyes on the road, convinced that if he didn't he'd lose control of himself and the car. The result might be a sort of femme fatality. His attraction towards Sally and Martha had not been wholly sexual. Yet he had never felt such purely animal attraction that this woman radiated. Maybe, he decided, she didn't know it. He glanced at her. There again, maybe she did.

It said a lot for the woman if she could take his mind so completely off his various problems.

"My name's Magdalen," she smiled. "A bit of a mouthful. What's yours?"

It was a relief to find someone here who didn't already know his name. He rejected the unliked Lee and said: "Bill—Bill Ward."

"Short and sweet," she said. "Not like mine."

He grunted vaguely, consciously fighting the emotions rising in him. There was a word for them. A simple word—short and sweet—lust. He rather liked it. He'd been somewhat repressed on his home world and had kept a tight censorship on his feelings. Here it was obviously different.

A little later, he gave in. He stopped the car and kissed her. He was surprised at the ease with which he did it. He forgot about the tranquilomats, about the M-A 19, about the fortress. He forgot about everything except her, and that was maybe why he did what he did.

It was as if he was drawn into yet another world—a private world where only he and she had an existence. An enclosed world consisting only of their desire and their need to satisfy it.

Afterwards he felt gloomy, regretful and guilty. He started the car savagely. He knew he shouldn't blame her, but he did. He'd wasted time. Minutes were valuable, even seconds. He'd wasted hours.

Beside him she took a headscarf from her bag and tied it over her hair. "You're in a hurry."

He pressed the accelerator as far down as he could.

"What's the problem?" she shouted as the engine thudded noisily.

"I've wasted too much time already. I'll drop you off wherever it is you want."

"Oh, fine. Just one of those things, eh?"

"I suppose so. It was my fault. I shouldn't have picked you up in the first place."

She laughed. It wasn't a nice laugh. It was a mocking laugh and it seemed to punch him in the stomach.

"Okay," he said, "okay."

He switched on the headlamps as dusk became night. There was no milometer on the dashboard so he didn't know how far they'd travelled, but he was sure it was more than sixty miles.

"Where is this town?" he said.

"Not much further." Her voice softened. "I'm sorry, Lee. But what *is* the matter?"

Something was wrong. He couldn't place it. He put it down to his own anger.

"You may not know it," he said, "but I suspect that nearly all the people living here are being deceived. Do you know the fortress?"

"You mean that big building on the rock wastes?"

"That's it. Well, there's a group of people there who are duping you and the rest in some way. They want to destroy practically the whole of the human race by a particularly nasty method—and they want me to do it for them."

"What's that?"

Briefly, he explained.

Again she laughed. "By the sound of it, you're a fool to fight this Man Without A Navel and his friends. You ought to throw in your lot with them. You could be top man."

"Aren't you angry?" he said in surprise. "Don't you believe me?"

"Certainly. I just don't share your attitude. I don't understand you turning down a chance when it's offered. I'd take it. As I said, you could be top man."

"I've already been top man," he said, "in a manner of speaking. On my own world. I don't want that kind of responsibility. All I want to do is save something from the mess I've made of civilization."

"You're a fool, Lee."

That was it. She shouldn't have known him as Lee but as Bill, the name he'd introduced himself by. He stopped the car suddenly and looked at her suspiciously. The truth was dawning on him and it made him feel sick at himself that he could have fallen for her trap.

"You're working for him, aren't you. The Man?"

"You seem to be exhibiting all the symptoms of persecution mania, Seward. You need a good psychiatrist." She spoke coolly and reached into her handbag. "I don't feel safe with you."

"It's mutual," he said. "Get out of the car."

"No," she said quietly. "I think we'll go all the way to the fortress together." She put both hands into her bag. They came out with two things. One was a half bottle of brandy.

The other was a gun.

"Evidently my delay tactics weren't effective enough," she mocked. "I thought they might not be, so I brought these. Get out, yourself, Seward."

"You're going to kill me?"

"Maybe."

"But that isn't what The Man wants, is it?"

She shrugged, waving the gun.

Trembling with anger at his own gullibility and impotence, he got out. He couldn't think clearly.

She got out, too, keeping him covered. "You're a clever man, Seward. You've worked out a lot."

"There are others here who know what I know."

"What do they know?"

"They know about the set-up—about the conditioning."

She came round the car towards him, shaking her head. Still keeping him covered, she put the brandy bottle down on the seat.

He went for the gun.

He acted instinctively, in the knowledge that this was his only chance. He heard the gun go off, but he was forcing her wrist back. He slammed it down on the side of the car. She yelled and dropped it. Then he did what he had never thought he could do. He hit her, a short, sharp jab under the chin. She crumpled.

He stood over her, trembling. Then he took her headscarf and tied her limp hands behind her. He dragged her up and dumped her in the back of the car. He leant down and found the gun. He put it in his pocket.

Then he got into the driving seat, still trembling. He felt something hard under him. It was the brandy bottle. It was what he needed. He unscrewed the cap and took a long drink.

His brain began to explode even as he reached for the ignition.

It seemed to crackle and flare like burning timber. He grabbed the door handle. Maybe if he walked around . . .

He felt his knees buckle as his feet touched the ground. He strained to keep himself upright. He forced himself to move round the car. When he reached the bonnet, the headlamps blared at him, blinded him.

They began to blink rapidly into his eyes. He tried to raise his hands and cover his eyes. He fell sideways, the light still blinking. He felt nausea sweep up and through him. He saw the car's licence plate in front of him.

YOU 099
YOU 100
YOU 101

He put out a hand to touch the plate. It seemed normal. Yet the digits were clocking up like the numbers on an adding machine.

Again his brain exploded. A slow, leisurely explosion that subsided and brought a delicious feeling of well-being.

Green clouds like boiled jade, scent of chrysanthemums. Swaying lilies. Bright lines of black and white in front of his eyes. He shut them and opened them again. He was looking up at the blind in his bedroom.

As soon as he realized he was back, Seward jumped off the bed and made for the bench where he'd left the half-finished tranquilomat. He remembered something, felt for the gun he'd taken off the girl. It wasn't there.

But he felt the taste of the brandy in his mouth. Maybe it was as simple as that, he thought. Maybe all he needed to get back was alcohol.

There was sure to be some alcohol in the lab. He searched through cupboards and drawers until he found some in a jar. He filled a vial and corked it. He took off his shirt and taped the vial under his armpit—that way he might be able to transport it from his world to the other one.

Then he got down to work.

Lenses were reassembled, checked. New filters went in and old ones came out. He adjusted the resonators and amplifiers. He was recharging the battery which powered the transistorized circuits, when he sensed the mob outside. He left the little machine on the bench and went to the control board. He flicked three switches down and then, on impulse, flicked them off again. He went back to the bench and unplugged

the charger. He took the machine to the window. He drew
the blind up.

It was a smaller mob than usual. Evidently some of them
had learned their lesson and were now avoiding the laboratory.

Far away, behind them, the sun glinted on a calm sea. He
opened the window.

There was one good way of testing his tranquilomat. He
rested it on the sill and switched it to ATTRACT. That was
the first necessary stage, to hold the mob's attention. A faint,
pleasant humming began to come from the machine. Seward
knew that specially shaped and coloured lenses were whirling
at the front. The mob looked up towards it, but only those in
the centre of the group were held. The others dived away,
hiding their eyes.

Seward felt his body tightening, growing cold. Part of him
began to scream for the M-A 19. He clung to the machine's
carrying handles. He turned a dial from Zero to 50. There
were 100 units marked on the indicator. The machine was
now sending at half-strength. Seward consoled himself that if
anything went wrong he could not do any more harm to their
ruined minds. It wasn't much of a consolation.

He quickly saw that the combined simulated brainwaves,
sonic vibrations and light patterns were having some effect on
their minds. But what was the effect going to be? They were
certainly responding. Their bodies were relaxing, their faces
were no longer twisted with insanity. But was the tranquilomat actually doing any constructive good—what it had been
designed to do? He upped the output to 75 degrees.

His hands began to tremble. His mouth and throat were
tight and dry. He couldn't keep going. He stepped back. His
stomach ached. His bones ached. His eyes felt puffy. He began to move towards the machine again. But he couldn't
make it. He moved towards the half-full ampoule of M-A 19
on the table. He filled the blunt hypodermic. He found a
vein. He was weeping as the explosions hit his brain.

Seven

This time it was different.

He saw an army of machines advancing towards him. An
army of malevolent hallucinomats. He tried to run, but a

thousand electrodes were clamped to his body and he could not move. From nowhere, needles entered his veins. Voices shouted SEWARD! SEWARD! SEWARD! The hallucino-mats advanced, shrilling, blinking, buzzing—*laughing*. The machines were laughing at him.

SEWARD!

Now he saw Farlowe's car's registration plate.

YOU 110

YOU 111

YOU 119

SEWARD!

Y O U !

SEWARD!

His brain was being squeezed. It was contracting, contract-ing. The voices became distant, the machines began to recede. When they had vanished he saw he was standing in a circular room in the centre of which was a low dais. On the dais was a chair. In the chair was the Man Without A Navel. He smiled at Seward.

"Welcome back, old boy," he said.

Brother Sebastian and the woman, Magdalen, stood close to the dais. Magdalen's smile was cool and merciless, seeming to anticipate some new torture that the Man and Brother Sebastian had devised.

But Seward was jubilant. He was sure his little tranquilo-mat had got results.

"I think I've done it," he said quietly. "I think I've built a workable tranquilomat—and, in a way, it's thanks to you. I had to speed my work up to beat you—and I did it!"

They seemed unimpressed.

"Congratulations, Seward," smiled the Man Without A Navel. "But this doesn't alter the situation, you know. Just because you *have* an antidote doesn't mean we have to use it."

Seward reached inside his shirt and felt for the vial taped under his arm. It had gone. Some of his confidence went with the discovery.

Magdalen smiled. "It was kind of you to drink the drugged brandy."

He put his hands in his jacket pocket.

The gun was back there. He grinned.

"What's he smiling at?" Magdalen said nervously.

"I don't know. It doesn't matter. Brother Sebastian, I be-

lieve you have finished work on your version of Seward's hyp-
nomat?"

"I have," said the sighing, cold voice.

"Let's have it in. It is a pity we didn't have it earlier. It
would have saved us time—and Seward all his efforts."

The curtains behind them parted and Mr Hand, Mr Morl and
the Laughing Cavalier wheeled in a huge, bizarre machine
that seemed to have a casing of highly-polished gold, silver
and platinum. There were two sets of lenses in its domed,
head-like top. They looked like eyes staring at Seward.

Was this a conditioning machine like the ones they'd probably used on the human populace? Seward thought it was
likely. If they got him with that, he'd be finished. He pulled
the gun out of his pocket. He aimed it at the right-hand lens
and pulled the trigger.

The gun roared and kicked in his hand, but no bullet left
the muzzle. Instead there came a stream of small, brightly
coloured globes, something like those used in the attraction
device on the tranquilomat. They sped towards the machine,
struck it, exploded. The machine buckled and shrilled. It
steamed and two discs, like lids, fell across the lenses. The
machine rocked backwards and fell over.

The six figures began to converge on him, angrily.

Suddenly, on his left, he saw Farlowe, Martha and Sally
step from behind a screen.

"Help me!" he cried to them.

"We can't!" Farlowe yelled. "Use your initiative, son!"

"Initiative?" He looked down at the gun. The figures were
coming closer. The Man Without A Navel smiled slowly.
Brother Sebastian tittered. Magdalen gave a low, mocking
laugh that seemed—strangely—to be a criticism of his sexual
prowess. Mr Morl and Mr Hand retained their mournful and
cheerful expressions respectively. The Laughing Cavalier flung
back his head and—laughed. All around them the screens,
which had been little more than head-high were lengthening,
widening, stretching up and up.

He glanced back. The screens were growing.

He pulled the trigger of the gun. Again it bucked, again it
roared—and from the muzzle came a stream of metallic-grey
particles which grew into huge flowers. The flowers burst into
flame and formed a wall between him and the six.

He peered around him, looking for Farlowe and the others.

He couldn't find them. He heard Farlowe's shout: "Good luck, son!" He heard Martha and Sally crying goodbye. "Don't go!" he yelled.

Then he realized he was alone. And the six were beginning to advance again—malevolent, vengeful.

Around him the screens, covered in weird designs that curled and swirled, ever-changing, were beginning to topple inwards. In a moment he would be crushed.

Again he heard his name being called. SEWARD! SEW-ARD!

Was it Martha's voice? He thought so.

"I'm coming," he shouted, and pulled the trigger again.

The Man Without A Navel, Magdalen, Brother Sebastian, the Laughing Cavalier, Mr Hand and Mr Morl—all screamed in unison and began to back away from him as the gun's muzzle spouted a stream of white fluid which floated into the air.

Still the screens were falling, slowly, slowly.

The white fluid formed a net of millions of delicate strands. It drifted over the heads of the six. It began to descend. They looked up and screamed again.

"Don't Seward," begged the Man Without A Navel. "Don't, old man—I'll make it worth your while."

Seward watched as the net engulfed them. They struggled and cried and begged.

It did not surprise him much when they began to shrink.

No! *They* weren't shrinking—he was growing. He was growing over the toppling screens. He saw them fold inwards. He looked down and the screens were like cards folding neatly over the six little figures struggling in the white net. Then, as the screens folded down, the figures were no longer in sight. It got lighter. The screens rolled themselves into a ball.

The ball began to take on a new shape.

It changed colour. And then, there it was—a perfectly formed human skull.

Slowly, horrifyingly, the skull began to gather flesh and blood and muscles to itself. The stuff flowed over it. Features began to appear. Soon, in a state of frantic terror, Seward recognized the face.

It was his own.

His own face, its eyes wide, its lips parted. A tired,
stunned, horrified face.

He was back in the laboratory. And he was staring into a
mirror.

He stumbled away from the mirror. He saw he wasn't holding a gun in his hand but a hypodermic needle. He looked
round the room.

The tranquilomat was still on the window-sill. He went to
the window. There, quietly walking among the ruins below,
was a group of sane men and women. They were still in rags,
still gaunt. But they were sane. That was evident. They were
saner than they had ever been before.

He called down to them, but they didn't hear him.

Time for that later, he thought. He sat on the bed, feeling
dazed and relieved. He dropped the needle to the floor, certain he wouldn't need to use it again.

It was incredible, but he thought he knew where he had
been. The final image of his face in the mirror had given him
the last clue.

He had been inside his own mind. The M-A 19 was merely
a hallucinogenic after all. A powerful one, evidently, if it
could give him the illusion of rope-marks on his wrists, bites
on his neck and the rest.

He had escaped into a dream world.

Then he wondered—but why? What good had it done?

He got up and went towards the mirror again.

Then he heard the voice. Martha's voice.

SEWARD! SEWARD! Seward, listen to me!

No, he thought desperately. No, it can't be starting again.
There's no need for it.

He ran into the laboratory, closing the door behind him,
locking it. He stood there, trembling, waiting for the withdrawal symptoms. They didn't come.

Instead he saw the walls of the laboratory, the silent computers and meters and dials, begin to blur. A light flashed on
above his head. The dead banks of instruments suddenly
came alive. He sat down in a big chrome, padded chair
which had originally been used for the treating of test-sub-
jects.

His gaze was caught by a whirling stroboscope that had appeared from nowhere. Coloured images began to form in

front of his eyes. He struggled to get up but he couldn't.

YOU 121

YOU 122

YOU 123

Then the first letter changed to a V.

VOU 127

SEWARD!

His eyelids fell heavily over his eyes.

"Professor Seward." It was Martha's voice. It spoke to someone else. "We may be lucky, Tom. Turn down the volume."

He opened his eyes.

"Martha."

The woman smiled. She was dressed in a white coat and was leaning over the chair. She looked very tired. "I'm not—Martha—Professor Seward. I'm Doctor Kalin. Remember?"

"Doctor Kalin, of course."

His body felt weaker than it had ever felt before. He leaned back in the big chair and sighed. Now he was remembering.

It had been his decision to make the experiment. It had seemed to be the only way of speeding up work on the development of the tranquilomats. He knew that the secret of a workable machine was imbedded in the deepest level of his unconscious mind. But, however much he tried—hypnosis, symbol-association, word-association—he couldn't get at it.

There was only one way he could think of—a dangerous experiment for him—an experiment which might not work at all. He would be given a deep-conditioning, made to believe that he had brought disaster to the world and must remedy it by devising a tranquilomat. Things were pretty critical in the world outside, but they weren't as bad as they had conditioned him to believe. Work on the tranquilomats *was* falling behind—but there had been no widespread disaster, *yet*. It was bound to come unless they could devise some means of mass-cure for the thousands of neurotics and victims of insanity. An antidote for the results of mass-tension.

So, simply, they conditioned him to think his efforts had destroyed civilization. He must devise a working tranquilomat. They had turned the problem from an intellectual one into a personal one.

The conditioning had apparently worked.

He looked around the laboratory at his assistants. They were all alive, healthy, a bit tired, a bit strained, but they looked relieved.

"How long have I been under?" he asked.

"About fourteen hours. That's twelve hours since the experiment went wrong."

"Went wrong?"

"Why, yes," said Doctor Kalin in surprise. "Nothing was happening. We tried to bring you round—we tried every darned machine and drug in the place—nothing worked. We expected catatonia. At least we've managed to save you. We'll just have to go on using the ordinary methods of research, I suppose." Her voice was tired, disappointed.

Seward frowned. But he *had* got the results. He knew exactly how to construct a working tranquilomat. He thought back.

"Of course," he said. "I was only conditioned to believe that the world was in ruins and I had done it. There was nothing about—about—the *other* world."

"What other world?" Macpherson, his Chief Assistant, asked the question.

Seward told them. He told them about the Man Without A Navel, the fortress, the corridors, the tortures, the landscapes seen from Farlowe's car, the park, the maze, the Vampire, Magdalen . . . He told them how, in what he now called Condition A, he had believed himself hooked on a drug called M-A 19.

"But we don't have a drug called M-A 19," said Doctor Kalin.

"I know that now. But I didn't know that and it didn't matter. I would have found something to have made the journey into—the other world—a world existing only in my skull. Call it Condition B, if you like—or Condition X, maybe. The unknown. I found a fairly logical means of making myself *believe* I was entering another world. That was M-A 19. By inventing symbolic characters who were trying to stop me, I made myself work harder. Unconsciously I knew that Condition A was going wrong—so I escaped into Condition B in order to put right the damage. By acting out the drama I was able to clear my mind of its confusion. I had, as I suspected, the secret of the tranquilomat somewhere down there all the time. Condition A failed to release that secret—Condition B succeeded. I can build you a workable tranquilomat, don't worry."

"Well," Macpherson grinned. "I've been told to use my imagination in the past—but you *really* used yours!"

"That was the idea, wasn't it? We'd decided it was no good just using drugs to keep us going. We decided to use our drugs and hallucinomats directly, to condition me to believe that what we feared will happen, *had* happened."

"I'm glad we didn't manage to bring you back to normality, in that case," Doctor Kalin smiled. "You've had a series of classic—if more complicated than usual—nightmares. The Man Without A Navel, as you call him, and his 'allies' symbolized the elements in you that were holding you back from the truth—diverting you. By 'defeating' the Man, you defeated those elements."

"It was a hell of a way to get results," Seward grinned. "But I got them. It was probably the only way. Now we can produce as many tranquilomats as we need. The problem's over. I've—in all modesty—" he grinned, "saved the world before it needed saving. It's just as well."

"What about your 'helpers', though," said Doctor Kalin helping him from the chair. He glanced into her intelligent, mature face. He had always liked her.

"Maybe," he smiled, as he walked towards the bench where the experimental tranquilomats were laid out, "maybe there was quite a bit of wish-fulfilment mixed up in it as well."

"It's funny how you didn't realize that it wasn't real, isn't it?" said Macpherson behind him.

"Why is it funny?" he turned to look at Macpherson's long, worn face. "Who knows what's real, Macpherson. This world? That world? Any other world? I don't feel so adamant about this one, do you?"

"Well . . ." Macpherson said doubtfully. "I mean, you're a trained psychiatrist as well as everything else. You'd think you'd recognize your own symbolic characters."

"I suppose it's possible." Macpherson had missed his point. "All the same," he added. "I wouldn't mind going back there some day. I'd quite enjoy the exploration. And I liked some of the people. Even though they were probably wish-fulfilment figures. Farlowe—father—it's possible." He glanced up as his eye fell on a meter. It consisted of a series of code-let-

ters and three digits. VOU 18 it said now. There was Farlowe's number-plate. His mind had turned the V into a Y.
He'd probably discover plenty of other symbols around,
which he'd turned into something else in the other world. He
still couldn't think of it as a dream world. It had seemed so
real. For him, it was still real.

"What about the woman—Martha?" Doctor Kalin said.
"You called *me* Martha as you were waking up."

"We'll let that one go for the time being," he grinned.
"Come on, we've still got a lot of work to do."

The Golden Barge

Day gave way to night, inevitably, for the fourth time since wide-mouthed Jephraim Tallow had begun his chase. He slept at the rudder of his boat, trusting to his luck, and the next morning he awoke to find himself soaked to the skin, but still on course. The yellow overalls he wore had not been made for use outdoors and they had given him little protection. He had not slept well, for his dreams had been scarlet dreams; but now that it was morning, he could forget. What was one man's life? How did a single murder matter when the golden barge, which was his goal, moved surely onwards?

The rain sliced down out of a grey sky, lancing into the waters of the river, spattering over the canvas of the boat. And a wind was beginning to blow. Instead of willows, rhododendrons now lined the banks of the river. They were heavy with the fallen water, sinking beneath its sodden weight. The wind was rising and bending the bushes into rustling nightmare beasts which reached out to tempt Tallow ashore. He laughed at them hysterically, and the wind filled his ship's sail, distending it until the mast creaked in unison with Tallow's laughter. But Tallow ceased to laugh when he realized his danger; realized that he had no cause for laughter, for the wind was driving his vessel towards the luring bushes. Frantically, he attempted to adjust the sail, but the rig of the stolen boat was unfamiliar and in his panic he succeeded only in tangling the knots into a worse mess. The wind blew stronger, bending the mast, swelling the sail like a cannibal's belly.

He tore at the knots until his fingers bled and his nails were broken shreds catching in the tackle. Then, as the wind increased, he had to concentrate on controlling the rudder in order to keep the boat on some kind of course. He saw that

107

he was nearing a bend in the river, and saw two other things: a white flash against the dark green mass of foliage and the golden barge just ahead, looming tall. With an effort, he calmed himself, realizing that in his panic he had not sighted his objective, the mysterious implacable barge. He had killed so that he should be able to follow it and now he dare not let it escape. He needed to stay on course just long enough to reach the barge and board her and he knew that he could but, even as his boat's prow gashed the waters in furious speed, he came to the bend in the river and his ship lurched and shuddered to a halt. He realized that he had run aground on one of the many hidden sand-bars which plagued river traffic.

Angry, and screaming his disappointment to the wind and the rain, Tallow leapt out into the shallow water and attempted to heave the ship off the bar as rain smote him in the face and flayed his skin. His efforts were useless. In a second, the barge had disappeared from his sight and he had sunk to his knees in the water, sobbing in frustration. The rain began to fall with lessening intensity and the velocity of the wind dropped, but still Tallow remained on his knees, bowed in the swirling, dirty water, his hands above him, gripping the sides of the boat. The rain and wind subsided and eventually the sun dissected the clouds. The sun shone on the boat, on Tallow, on the river, on bushes and trees and on a white house, five storeys high, which gleamed like the newly-washed face of a child.

Tallow lifted red eyes and sighed. He tried once more to move the boat, but could not. He looked around him. He saw the house. He would need help. With a shrug, he splashed knee-deep through the water, to the bank, climbing up its damp, crumbling, root-riddled earth and cursing his luck.

Tallow, in some ways, was a fatalist, and his fatalism at last came to the rescue of his sanity as ahead of him he saw a wall of red-brick, patched with black moss-growths. His mood changed almost instantly and he was once again his old, cold cocky self. For beyond the wall he could see the head and shoulders of a woman. The barge could wait for a little while.

She was a sharp-jawed, pout-lipped beauty and her eyes were green as scum. She wore a battered felt hat and stared at Tallow over the short stone wall which reached almost to her shoulder.

She smiled at him. One of her delightfully even teeth was stained brown; two others were green, matching her eyes.

Tallow's senses for women had been dormant to the point of atrophy for years. Now he savoured the knowledge that he was going to form an attachment for this one. For the moment, he hugged the knowledge to himself.

"Good morning, madam," he said, straddling his legs and making a low, ungainly bow. "My sloop ran aground and I'm stranded."

"Then you must stay with me," she smiled again and put her head to one side by way of emphasizing the invitation. "That's my house over there." She stretched a rounded arm and pointed. Her fingers were long and delicate, terminating in purple-painted talons. The house was the big white one Tallow had seen.

"A fine house it is, too, madam, by the looks of it." Tallow swaggered towards the low wall.

"It is fine," she admitted. "But rather empty. I have only two servants."

"Not enough," Tallow frowned. "Not enough." He could always catch the barge up, he thought. He vaulted the wall. This was a remarkable feat for one of his slight stature, and he achieved it with a delicacy and grace normally alien to him. He stood beside her. He looked at her from beneath half-closed lids. "I would be grateful for a bed for the night," he said. "And help in the morning. My ship must be re-floated."

"I will arrange it," she promised. She had mobile lips which moved smoothly around the words as she spoke. She was slim-waisted and full-hipped. Her bottom was round and firm beneath the skirt of yellow wool. Her large breasts pushed at the shining silk of a black blouse and the heels of her shoes were six inches long. She turned and headed for the house. "Follow me," she said.

Tallow followed, marvelling at the way she kept her balance on her high heels. Without them, he thought gleefully, she was only an inch or so taller than he. She led him through the garden of spear-like leaves, finally arriving at a sandy road which wound towards the house.

A two-wheeled carriage stood empty, drawn by a bored

donkey. The woman's flesh was soft and it itched at Tallow's fingertips as he helped her into the carriage, doing mental somersaults all the while. He grinned to himself as he got in beside her and took the reins.

"Gee up!" he shouted. The donkey sighed, and moved foward at a tired shuffling trot.

Five minutes later, Tallow tugged hard at the donkey's reins and brought the cart to a crunching-halt on the gravel outside the house. A flight of solid stone steps led up to big timber doors which were half-open. "My home," the woman remarked superfluously and Tallow felt a disappointed shock at this inanity; but the feeling soon passed as it was replaced by his glee for his good fortune.

"Your home!" he yelled. "Hurrah!" He didn't bother to mask his emotions any more. He bounced out of the carriage and helped her from it. Her legs were well-shaped and trim. She smiled and laughed and treated him to a gorgeous display of brown, green and white. They climbed the steps together, leaping up them like ballet-dancers, with their feet clattering in time. Her hand slipped into his as they pushed the door open and marched into a hall with rafters lost in gloom. It was a shadowy hall, hushed as a church. Dust flew in a single beam of sunlight which entered by way of the door which was apparently warped, for it didn't shut completely. Dust swirled into Tallow's nostrils and he sneezed. She laughed delightfully.

"My name's Pandora," she told him loudly. "What's yours?"

"Tallow," he replied, his eyes watering and his nose still itching. "Jephraim Tallow, at your service!"

"At my service!" She clapped her hands and the echoes reverberated around the hall. "At my service!" She clapped and laughed until the hall resounded with the applause and laughter of a vast audience.

A voice, like the last trumpet, boomed and crashed into Tallow's startled ear-drums. "Do you require me, madam?"

Staring through the gloom as the last echo fluttered in distant corners, Tallow was surprised to see that the hollow trumpet voice emanated from a bent and wizened ancient, clad in faded finery of gold and silver, tarnished and varnished with long years of wear. Pandora answered the servant: "Dinner, Fench!" she cried. "Dinner for two—and make it good!"

"Yes, madam." With a swirl of dust, the bent one vanished through a barely discernible door.

"One of my servants," whispered Pandora confidingly. She frowned. "The other one's his wife—damn her!" She cursed quite viciously; softly and sibilantly, like a snake spitting. Tallow, knowing nothing of the place, wondered how an old woman could arouse such wrath in Pandora. But a thousand reasons swam into his head and he rejected them all. He was not a man to jump to conclusions. Conclusions were too final—they led to death. She clutched his hand and led him through the hall to where wide oak stairs twisted upwards. "Come, Jephraim," she murmured. "Come my tender Tallow, and let us get you dressed!"

Tallow recovered his self-confidence and rushed like a rabbit up the stairway, his long legs stepping high. They polka'd hand in hand to the third floor of the vast, dark house. Their hair, his red, hers black as jet, flew behind them and they laughed all the while, happily, insensitive to everything but themselves.

Up to the third floor they bounded, and she led him to a door, one of a number, as solid as its fellows. He was slightly out of breath, for he was not used to climbing so many stairs. As she strained to turn the knob on the door, using both hands, bending her body and screwing up her face until eventually the door creaked open, he began to hiccup.

Meanwhile, the wind which had driven Tallow on to the sand bar was howling around the golden barge as it pushed calmly towards whatever victories or dooms awaited it.

"Jephraim," whispered Pandora, as he sat back in his chair, sipping brandy from a glass as big as his head.

He grunted questioningly, smiling foolishly. The meal had been liberally diluted with night-red wine.

"Jephraim—where are you from?" She leant forward across the small table. She had changed into a dress of dark, sentient blue which flowed off her smooth shoulders to cascade like dangerous ice down her body, to flare suddenly at the knees. She wore two rings on her left hand; sapphires and emeralds—and around her soft throat hung a thin chain of gold. Tallow's new emotions were rioting through him and a childish awe for his good fortune still stuck in part of his mind, even as he stretched out a hand and groped for Pandora's taloned fingers. Pinpricks of excitement and antici-

pation were becoming too much to bear and his voice
throbbed as he spoke, echoing his heart-beats.

"From a town many miles away," he said, and this appeared to satisfy her.

"Where were you going, Jephraim?" This question was
asked idly, as if she didn't expect him to answer.

"I was—I am—following a golden ship which passed your
house just before I ran aground. Did you see it?"

She laughed, and her laughter hurt him causing him to
withdraw his hand. "Silly Tallow," she cried. "No such ship
passed—and I didn't see it for I was in the garden a long
while—watching the river. I never miss the ships."

"You missed this one," he muttered, glaring into his glass.

"Your jokes are hard to understand, Jephraim," she said
more softly. "But I'm sure I'll like them—when we know
each other better." Her voice dropped lower and lower until
it was almost inaudible, but the timbre of it was enough to
churn Tallow's thoughts into other channels almost immediately. Some of his self-assurance, so badly shattered recently,
returned to him and he folded his ten fingers around the
brandy glass, lifted it, and poured the entire contents down
his throat. He smacked his lips and gasped, then put the glass
down with a bang, clattering the dirty cutlery.

He wiped his mouth on the back of his hand, the scarlet
sleeve of his new corduroy jacket somewhat impeding this action, and looked around the small candle-lit room until it
blurred. Pettishly, he shook his head to clear it and, support-
ing himself with hands spread on the table, stood up. He
looked intently into her eyes and she smiled hesitantly.

"Pandora, I love you." He was relieved now that it was
over.

"Good," she purred. "That makes it so much easier."

Tallow was too drunk to wonder what it was which would
be easier. He ignored the statement and rocked towards her.
She stood up, slowly, carefully, and glided towards him. He
gathered her in and kissed her throat. As she was standing
up, he couldn't quite reach her mouth. Her breasts pushed
against his chest and her arms slid up his back, one hand
caressing the nape of his neck. The other hand moved star-
tingly down his back and around his hip.

"Ouch!" he moaned a moment later. "That ring hurts!"
She pouted, then smiled, and took her rings off. He wriggled
in his tight, black velvet trousers and wished that he were

naked. "Shall we go to bed, now?" she shrugged at just the right moment.

"Yes," agreed Tallow with earnest certainty. "Yes." She supported his reeling body as they left the room and made their way up the flight of stairs to her own bedroom.

A week throbbed by. A bedded week, wearing for Tallow, but delightful. Pandora's expert lessons had taught him, among other things, that he was a man; a man, to boot, who had learned to please Pandora. The week had taught him something else, something subtler, and he now had a tighter rein on his emotions; could control both appetite and expression to a greater degree.

Tallow lay in bed beside a sleeping Pandora, attempting to shift the sheet which covered her. His eyes were as yet unsatiated by the sight of her lying naked and at his mercy. The truth was, he had to admit, that for the most part he was inextricably at her mercy. But Pandora was a woman, and took only the right and honest advantage of her superior position. Tallow remained in love with her and the love grew strongly and he was content. Her yielding and her occasional pleas were rare, but could be savoured for their rarity. Weariness, however, was encroaching to make a wreck of Tallow. He slept longer, made love a trifle less violently, though with more skill, and even now, after ten hours of sleep, he did not feel rested, but none the less, he was content. He felt happiness and sometimes sadness when Pandora unknowingly outraged him, but the joy far outweighed the pain.

He had just laid bare her breasts, when she awoke. She blinked and then opened her eyes as widely as she could, looked at him, looked down and gently drew the sheet back towards her chin. Tallow grunted his disappointment, raised himself on one elbow, cushioned his head in his hand, and stared down at her.

"Good morning," he said with mock accusation.

" 'Morning, Jephraim." She smiled like a schoolgirl, stirring tenderness and desire in him. He flung himself upon her in a flurry of sheeting. She laughed, gasped, was silent for some seconds, and then kissed him.

"I earned it, didn't I?" she said, staring into his eyes.

"You did," he rolled over and sat up in bed.

"You need me, don't you?" she said softly, behind him.

"Yes," he said, and then paused, thinking—he had answered the question too quickly. Before he had considered it again properly, he had said: "At least—I think so."

Her voice was still soft, unchanged; "What do you mean—you think so?"

"Sorry," he smiled, turning towards her and looking down at her. "Sorry—I don't know what I meant."

She frowned then, and shifted in the bed. "I don't know either," she said. "I don't know what you mean. What did you mean?"

"I've told you," he said, deciding that he was a fool. "I don't know."

She turned over on her side, towards the wall, away from him. "Either you need me or you don't."

"That's not strictly true," Tallow sighed. "I can need you—and I can't. There are things to need at certain times. I need you sometimes." I'm right, he thought—for it was clear to him now and it had never been so, before.

She was silent.

"It's true, Pandora," he knew that he should stop. "Surely you see that it's true.

"Love isn't everything," he mumbled lamely, feeling uncertain and beaten.

"Isn't it?" Her voice was muffled and cold.

"No!" he said, anger coming to his rescue. He got up, pulled on his clothes and walked over to the window, viciously tearing back the curtains. It was raining outside. He could see the river in the distance. He stood by the window for a few seconds and then turned back to stare at the bed. Pandora still faced the wall and he couldn't see her expression.

He stamped from the room, on his way to the bathroom. He felt troubled and annoyed, but he couldn't analyse the feeling. He knew, somehow, that he was right; knew that he shouldn't have spoken to her as he had, but was glad, also that he had done so. The floor was cold to his bare feet as he walked, and he could hear the rain beating to the ground and on to the roof. It was a drab, unsettled day and fitting for his mood.

At breakfast, she soon got over her former temper and, for the moment at least, they had forgotten their earlier conflict.

"What shall we do, today, Jephraim?" she said, putting down her coffee cup.

In a half-dream, not really aware of what he was saying, Tallow answered on the spur of the moment: "Ride! That's what we'll do! You have some horses, I've seen them."

"I have—but I didn't know you could ride."

"I can't," he grinned. "I can't, sweetheart, but I can learn!"

"Of course you can!" She was now in his mood. "But what shall we do about the rain?"

"To hell with the rain—it can't affect us. Come, love—to horse!" He galloped like an idiot from the breakfast-room. Laughing, she ran after him.

They rode all through the day, stopping sometimes to eat and to make love when the sun shone. They rode, and after two uncertain hours, Tallow soon learned how to sit his mare and to guide her. He was still an amateur, but a fast learner. Since the night he had seen the barge, he had been learning many things, quickly. Ideas rushed into his open, greedy mind and he gratefully absorbed them. So they rode through the rain and the sunshine and they laughed and loved together, forgetful of anything else; Tallow with his tiny frame and long legs, perched high above the ground on a chestnut mare; Pandora, petite and voracious for his attention, sometimes gay, often enigmatic, always honest; Pandora, a woman.

They rode for hours until at last they came to a stretch of the river upstream, which Tallow had passed a week earlier when asleep. They came to a hill and breathless and excited, fell into one another's arms, dovetailed together, and sank on to the damp turf, careless and carefree.

"Your river," whispered Pandora, some time later. "I'll always think of it as yours, now. I used to think it was mine, but I know it isn't."

Tallow was puzzled. He said: "It's everyone's river—that's the beauty of it. Everyone's."

"No," she said. "It's yours—I know."

"It's not just mine, darling," he said tenderly. "Anyone can sail on it, bathe in it, drink from it. That's why it's there."

"Perhaps," she compromised at last. "Perhaps it is, but I know what I shall always think. The river is your life."

"One day, I may make you a present of it, sweetheart," he smiled, and he was right, though he didn't know it.

He stared at the river and then, just for a fleeting moment, he saw the golden barge, sailing calmly, as it always did, unruffled. He turned to her, pointing. "There!" he cried excitedly. "There—now you see I wasn't joking! The golden ship!" But when he looked again, it had gone and Pandora was getting up, walking towards the horses.

"You always spoil things," she said. "You always say something to worry me."

In silence, they rode away from the river and Tallow thought carefully of the barge and Pandora.

Later that night, the rift unhealed, they sat in front of the dining-room fire, morosely drinking. She was truculent, unapproachable, he was turbulent, wondering if, after all, the things he wanted were so unattainable. So they sat, until there was a disturbance outside and Tallow went to the window to see what was happening. It was dark and he couldn't see much. The night was a confusion of laughter and screams, flickering torches and shifting shadows. Tallow saw that a drunken group was coming towards the house. He welcomed the interruption.

"Visitors," he said. "Revellers."

"I don't want to see them."

"Why not—we could have a party or something?"

"Shut up!" she pouted.

He sighed and went downstairs into the dark, cold, draughty hall. By the time he reached it, people were thumping on the half-open door.

"Is anyone in?"

"Shelter for some poor weary travellers, I beg thee!"

Laughter.

"Are you sure this house belongs to someone?" A woman's voice, this. Answered by another woman: "Yes, dear, I saw a light in an upstairs window."

"Is anyone home?"

"We've got plenty of bottles!"

Laughter again.

Tallow pulled the door back and stood confronting the interlopers, who worried him. They represented a threat which he could not define. "Good evening," he said, belligerently now.

"Good evening, my dear sir, good evening to you!" A grinning, patronizing corpulence, swathed in extravagant clothing, a cloak, knee-length boots, a top-hat, bearing a silver-worked cane and bowing theatrically.

"Can I help you?" said Tallow, hoping that he couldn't.

"We're lost." The man was drunk. He swayed towards Tallow and stared at him intently, his breath stinking of alcohol. "We're lost, and have nowhere to go! Can you put us up?"

"This isn't my house," said Tallow in stupefaction. "I'll see. You'd better come in anyway. How'd you get this far?"

"By boat—boats—lots of boats. Fun. Until we got lost, that is."

"All right," Tallow walked back up the stairs and rejoined Pandora. She was still sulking.

"Who is it?" she said petulantly. "Tell them to go away and let's get to bed."

"I agree, dearest," Tallow's mood changed to its former state and his quick tongue babbled, though he didn't mean what he said. "But we can't turn them away—they're lost. They can sleep here—won't bother us, will they?"

"I suppose I'd better see them, Jephraim," she got up, kissed him and together, warmly, arm in arm, they went downstairs.

The revellers' torches were still burning, turning the dusty hall into a madly dancing inferno of leaping light and shuddering shadow. As the fat leader saw Pandora and Tallow descend the stairs, he leered at Pandora. "The lady of the house!" he bawled to his friends, and they laughed, uneasily; he was embarrassing them now. The noise in the dusty cavern of a hall became a zoo-like cacophony.

Pandora said politely, but without feeling: "You may stay the night here, if you wish. We have plenty of beds." She turned to go upstairs.

"Beds!"

The drunken mob took up the word gleefully, chanting it round the hall. "Beds. Beds. Beds." After a short while, the sound became even more meaningless and they subsided into high-pitched laughter. Pandora and Tallow stood observing them. "Let's have some light, Jephraim," she suggested.

With a shrug, Tallow reluctantly borrowed a torch from a reveller and began to ignite the wicks of the candles. The hall erupted with light, dazzling the occupants. Again the giggling began. In the centre of the hall was a long table, chairs lining the walls. This was the first time Tallow had seen the room lighted. Grime was everywhere and the paint was peeling. Mildew had formed in patches on the ceiling and walls and the light only served to pick it out. Tallow

shrugged and moved to return upstairs again, but Pandora
put her hand on his arm. "We'll stay for a short while," she
said. I wish she'd made up her mind, he thought glumly, now
regretting the impulse which had driven him to allow the
people admission. They were soft, these people, soft beyond
Tallow's experience, pampered darlings to the last; slim,
brittle-eyed women and fat, blank-eyed men, bewilderingly
running over the surface of life, discontent with their own
fear-moulded values and afraid to find new ones, fooling
themselves that they were alive. Tallow could only pity them
and loathe what they represented. Every second they remained, they drove him into himself, retreating into the em-
bracing depths of his own dark soul.

He continued to stare at them from out of his skull; continued to stare as bottles were piled on the table and Pandora
was lost among the others, absorbed into their shallowness.
Tallow was vaguely terrified then, but his mind refused to
control his body as he stood on the stairs watching them, unable to leave or to join them. Clothes were flung in all directions and Tallow saw a blue dress and a black cape flutter
outwards together. Naked bellies wobbled and naked breasts
bounced, and white unhealthy flesh was a background for
dark hair. Tallow felt ill. At last his feet dragged him upwards back to the bedroom. His ego had been shattered; but
the pain of his loss, of his humiliation, was greater. He lay on
the bed, sobbing; thoughtless and emotionful, his whole world
a timeless flood of self-pity.

He lay, his head throbbing and aching, for hours; eventually falling into a fitful slumber which lasted another hour.
When he eventually awoke, he was calm. He knew that he had
done wrong, had destroyed part of himself in denying the
barge for Pandora's love—or his own love for Pandora. He
had delayed too long, and the barge should be followed, if
there was still time. That was his aim, his goal, his function in
life—to follow the barge and to go where it led him, im-
material of what other things distracted him. He got a large
woollen cloak from the cupboard and put it around his shoulders. Then he left, perturbed that he would have to pass
through the hall on his way out. When he reached it, he was
astounded.

In the centre of the room was a pulsating pyramid of flesh;

clean flesh and dirty flesh; soft flesh and rough flesh. It was ludicrous. There were limbs of all descriptions in most peculiar juxtaposition. A pair of pink buttocks seemed to spring an arm; noses lay upon legs, eyes peered from beneath genitals, faces or torsos, breasts upon toes. Such a scene might have disgusted Tallow, instead he was bewildered, for the strangest sight of all was the arm which waved at the top of the throbbing human mountain. It clutched a corruscating wineglass. The fingers were purple-painted talons; Pandora's fingers. Every so often the arm would disappear into the pile and the glass would return, less full, held like Liberty's torch, to its place above the pyramid. Tallow swallowed, his eyes wide. On tip-toe, his bitterness surging inside him once more, he circumnavigated the heap and pulled on the door.

"Goodnight, Pandora," he called as he left.

The wineglass waved. "Goodnight, Jephraim, see you later!" The voice was muffled and slurred, tinged with a false gaiety which was not like honest Pandora at all; normally she was either happy or sad or troubled, never false in her feelings.

"No you won't, Pandora," he shouted as he at last pulled the door open and fled into the rain-sodden night, blindly running down the sandy path, towards the river. Running from something which remained inside him, which he couldn't flee from, which was destroying him and which he was powerless to combat. So Tallow fled.

The boat was still on the sand-bar, half-full of rainwater. Tallow looked at it dispiritedly. Then, with a shrug, he took off his cloak and lowered his legs into the cold, murky water. He shivered, tensed and forced himself forward. The boat's timber felt good to his hands as he hoisted himself into it. He stared through the gloom, searching for the baling pans. At last he found them and began baling the water over the side.

When he had finished, he swung into the water again and slowly made his way round the ship, inspecting it as much as he could in the dim moonlight. Then he returned to the stern and put his shoulder to it, heaving. The boat shifted slightly. He moved round to the port side and began rocking it, shifting some of the compressed sand.

Three hours later, the boat was afloat. Weary with his effort, he sank into it and lay on the wet boards, half-asleep. He eventually arose when he heard someone moving about on the shore. Levering himself upright, he looked over the side and saw Pandora standing there, framed against the moonlight, her hair wild and ruffled by the wind, a man's dark cloak around her.

"Jephraim," she said, "I'm sorry—I don't know how it happened."

Tallow, his heart heavy in him, his mind dull, said: "That's all right, Pandora. I'm going now, anyway."

"Because of—that?" She pointed back to the house.

"No," he said slowly, "at least, not just because of that. It helped."

"Take me with you," she repeated humbly. "I'll do whatever you want."

He was perturbed. "Don't, Pandora—don't lose your respect for my sake." He was shaking out the sail. "Goodbye!" But she flung herself into the water and grasped the side of the boat, pulling herself into it with desperate strength. "Go back, Pandora!" he shouted, seeing his doom in her action. "Go back—go back! It's finished—you'll destroy me and yourself!" She made her way towards him, flinging her bedraggled body at his feet in horrible and uncharacteristic humility. "Take me!" she moaned.

The boat was now in midstream, making swiftly away from the bank.

"Oh, God, Pandora," he sobbed. "Don't make me—I must follow the barge."

"I'll come, Jephraim, darling. I'll come with you."

Tears painted his face in gleaming trails, he was breathing quickly, his brain in tumult, a dozen emotions clashing together, making him powerless for any action save speech.

He gave in suddenly, ashamed for her degradation. He sank down beside her, taking her wet, heaving body in his arms and in sympathy with her grief. And so, locked together in their fear and bewilderment, they slept.

Dawn was vicious, cloudless, bright. Tallow's eyes ached. Pandora still remained in troubled slumber, but she was on the borderline of wakefulness. As she sighed and began to struggle towards consciousness, an overpowering feeling of pity for her welled up in him. Then he looked down the river where it stretched straight into the horizon. Gold glimmered. Tallow acted. It was now or never.

He picked her up in his arms. She smiled in her sleep, loving him. He wrenched her away from him and hurled her outwards—hurled her into the river.

She screamed suddenly, in horror, as realization came.

Wolf

Whose little town are you, friend? Who owns you here? Wide and strong, you have an atmosphere of detached impermanence as you sit in the shallow valley with your bastion of disdainful pines surrounding you: with your slashed, gashed earth roads and your gleaming graveyards, cool under the sun. Here I stand in your peaceful centre, among the low houses, looking for your owner. Night is looming in my mind's backwaters.

I stop a long-jawed man with down-turned, sensuous lips. He rocks on his feet and stares at me in silence, his grey eyes brooding.

"Who owns this town?" I ask him.

"The people," he says. "The residents."

I laugh at the joke, but he refuses to join me, does not even smile. "Seriously—tell me. Who owns this town?"

He shrugs and walks off. I laugh louder: "Who owns this town, friend? Who owns it?" Does he hate me?

Without a mood, what is a man, anyway? A man has to have some kind of mood, even when he dreams. Scornfully, I laugh at the one who refused to smile and I watch his back as he walks stiffly and self-consciously over a bridge of wood and metal which spans soft water, full of blossom and leaves, flowing in the sunlight.

In my hand is a cool silver flask loaded with sweet fire. I know it is there. I lift it to my mouth and consume the fire, letting it consume me, also. Blandly, we destroy each other, the fire and I.

My stomach is full of flame and my legs are tingling, as soft as soda water, down to where my feet ache. *Don't leave me, sweetheart, with your hair of desire and your mockeries hollow in the moaning dawn. Don't leave me with the salt rain pushing down my cold face.* I laugh again and repeat the man's words: "The people—the residents!" Ho ho ho! But there is no one to hear my laughter now unless there are inhabitants in the white town's curtained dwellings. *Where are you, sweetheart—where's your taunting body, now, and the taste of your fingernails in my flesh?*

Harsh smoke drowns my sight and the town melts as I fall slowly down towards the cobbles of the street and a pain begins to inch its way through my stinging face.

Where's the peace that you seek in spurious godliness of another man—a woman? Why is it never there?

I regain my sight and look upwards to where the blue sky fills the world until it is obscured by troubled sounds which flow from a lovely face dominated by eyes asking questions which make me frustrated and angry, since I cannot possibly answer them. Not one of them. I smile, in spite of my anger and say, cynically: "It makes a change, doesn't it?" The girl shakes her head and the worried noises still pour from her mouth. Lips as red as blood—splashed on slender bones, a narrow, delicate skull. "Who—? Why are you—? What happened to you?"

"That's a very personal question, my dear," I say patronizingly. "But I have decided not to resent it."

"Thank you," says she. "Are you willing to rise and be helped somehow?"

Of course I am, but I would not let her know just yet. "I am seeking a friend who came this way," I say. "Perhaps you know her? She is fat with my life—full of my soul. She should be easy to recognize."

"No—I haven't . . ."

"Ah—well, if you happen to notice her, I would appreciate it if you would let me know. I shall be in the area for a short while. I have become fond of this town." A thought strikes me; "Perhaps you own it?"

"No."

"Please excuse the question if you are embarrassed by it. I, personally, would be quite proud to own a town like this. Is it for sale, do you think?"

"Come, you'd better get up. You might be arrested. Up you get."

There is a disturbing reluctance on the part of the residents to tell me the owner of the town. Of course, I could not afford to buy it—I asked cunningly, in the hope of discovering who the owner was. Maybe she is too clever for me. The idea is not appealing.

"You're like a dead bird," she smiles, "with your wings broken."

I refuse her hand and get up quickly. "Lead the way."

She frowns and then says: "Home I think." So off we go with her walking ahead. I point upwards: "Look—there's a cloud the shape of a cloud!" She smiled and I feel encouraged to such a degree that I want to thank her.

We reach her house with its green door opening directly on to the street. There are windows with red and yellow curtains and the white paint covering the stone is beginning to flake. She produces a key, inserts it into the large black iron lock and pushes the door wide open, gesturing gracefully for me to enter before her. I incline my head and walk into the darkened hallway of the house. It smells of lavender and is full of old polished oak and brass plates, horse-brasses, candlesticks with no candles in them. On my right is a staircase which twists up into gloom, the stairs covered by dark red carpet.

There are ferns in vases, placed on high shelves. Several vases of ferns are on the window-sill by the door.

"I have a razor if you wish to shave," she informs me. Luckily for her, I am self-critical enough to realize that I need a shave. I thank her and she mounts the stairs, wide skirt swinging, leading me to the upstairs floor and a small bathroom smelling of perfume and disinfectant.

She switches on the light. Outside, the blue of the sky is deepening and the sun has already set. She shows me the safety-razor, soap, towel. She turns a tap and water gushes out into her cupped hand. "Still hot," she says, turning and closing the door behind her. I am tired and make a bad job of shaving. I wash my hands as an afterthought and then go to the door to make sure it isn't locked. I open the door and peer out into the lighted passage. I shout: "Hey!" and her head eventually comes into sight around another door at the far end of the passage. "I've shaved."

"Go downstairs into the front room," she says. "I'll join you there in a few minutes." I grin at her and my eyes tell her that I know she is naked beneath her clothes. They all are. Without their clothes and their hair, where would they be? *Where is she? She came this way—I scented her trail right here, to this town. She could be hiding inside this*

*woman—fooling me. She was always clever in her own way.
I'll break her other hand, listen to the bones snap, and they
won't catch me. She sucked my life out of me and they
blamed me for breaking her fingers. I was just trying to get at
the ring I gave her. It was hidden by the blaze of the others.*

She turned me into a sharp-toothed wolf.

I thunder down the stairs, deliberately stamping on them,
making them moan and creak. I locate the front room and
enter it. Deep leather chairs, more brass, more oak, more
ferns in smoky glass of purple and scarlet. A fireplace without a fire. A soft carpet, multicoloured. A small piano with
black-and-white keys and a picture in a frame on top of it.

There is a white-clothed table with cutlery and plates for
two. Two chairs squat beside the table.

I stand with my back to the fireplace as I hear her
pointed-heeled shoes tripping down the stairs. "Good evening," I say politely when she comes in, dressed in a tight
frock of dark blue velvet, with rubies around her throat and
at her ears. There are dazzling rings on her fingers and I
shudder, but manage to control myself.

"Please sit down." She repeats the graceful gesture of the
hand, indicating a leather chair with a yellow cushion. "Do
you feel better now?" I am suspicious and will not answer
her. It might be a trick question, one never knows. "I'll get
dinner," she tells me, "I won't be long." Again I've defeated
her. She can't win at this rate.

I consume the foreign meal greedily and only realize afterwards that it might have been poisoned. Philosophically I re-
flect that it is too late now as I wait for coffee. I will test the
coffee and see if it smells of bitter almonds. If it does, I will
know it contains poison. I try to remember if any of the food
I have already eaten tasted of bitter almonds. I don't think
so. I feel comparatively safe.

She brings in the coffee smoking in a big brown earth-
enware pot. She sits down and pours me a cup. It smells good
and, relievedly, I discover it does not have the flavour of bitter almonds. Come to think of it, I am not altogether sure
what bitter almonds smell like.

"You may stay the night here, if you wish. There is a spare
room."

"Thank you," I say, letting my eyes narrow in a subtle
question, but she looks away from me and reaches a slim

hand for the coffee pot. "Thank you," I repeat. She doesn't answer me. What's her game? She takes a breath, is about to say something, looks quickly at me, changes her mind, says nothing. I laugh softly, leaning back in my chair with my hand clasped around my coffee cup.

"There are wolves and there are sheep," I say, as I have often said. "Which do you think you are?"

"Neither," says she.

"Then you are sheep," say I. "The wolves know what they are—what their function is. I am wolf."

"Really," she says and it is obvious that she is bored by my philosophy, not understanding it. "You had better go to bed now—you are tired."

"If you insist," I say lightly. "Very well."

She shows me up to the room overlooking the unlit street and bids me good night. Closing the door, I listen carefully for the sound of a key turning, but the sound doesn't come. The room contains a high, old-fashioned bed, a standard lamp, with a parchment shade with flowers pressed between two thicknesses, an empty bookcase and a wooden chair, beautifully carved. I feel the chair with my fingertips and shiver with delight at the sensation I receive. I pull back the quilt covering the bed and inspect the sheets which are clean and smell fresh. There are two white pillows, both very soft. I extract myself from my suit, taking off my shoes and socks and leaving my underpants on. I switch off the light and, trembling a little, get into the sheets. I am soon asleep, but it is still very early. I am convinced that I shall wake up at dawn.

I open my eyes in the morning and pale sunshine forces its way between gaps in the curtains. I lie in bed trying to go back to sleep, but cannot. I push away the covers, which have slipped partly off the bed, and get up. I go to the window and look down into the street.

Incredibly, a huge hare is loping along the pavement, its nose twitching. A lorry roars past, its gears grating, but the hare continues its imperturbable course. I am tensed, excited. I open my door and run along the passage to the woman's room, entering with a rush. She is asleep, one arm sprawled outwards, the hand dangling over the edge of her bed, her shoulders pale and alive. I take hold of one shoulder in a strong grip designed to hurt her into wakefulness. She cries out, sits up quivering.

"Quick," I say—"Come and see. There is a hare in the street!"

"Go away and let me sleep," she tells me, "let me sleep."

"No! You must come and look at the big hare in the street. How did it get there?"

She rises and follows me back to my room. I leap towards the window and see with relief that the hare is still there. "Look!" I point towards it and she joins me at the window. She, too, is amazed. "Poor thing," she gasps. "We must save it."

"Save it?" I am astounded. "Save it? No, I will kill it and we can eat it."

She shudders. "How could you be so cruel?" The hare disappears around a corner of the street. I am furious and all the nerves of my body are taut. "It has gone!"

"It will probably be all right," she says in a self-conciliatory tone and this makes me more angry. I begin to sob with frustration. She puts a hand on my arm. "What is the matter?" I shrug off the hand, then think better of it, I begin to cry against her breast. She pats me on the back and I feel better. "Let me come to bed with you," I plead.

"No," she says quietly. "You must rest."

"Let me sleep with *you*," I insist, but she breaks from my grasp and backs towards the door. "No! Rest."

I follow her, my eyes hot in my skull, my body full. "You owe me something," I tell her viciously. "You all do."

"Go away," she says threateningly, desperate and afraid of me. I continue to move toward her, beyond the door, along the passage. She starts to run for her room but I run also, and catch her. I catch her before she reaches the room. She screams. I clutch at her fingers. I bend them back slowly, putting my other hand over her mouth to stop her horrible noises. The bones snap in the slim, pale flesh. Not all at once.

"You made me wolf." I snarl. "And sheep must die." My teeth seek her pounding jugular, my nose scents the perfume of her throat. I slide my sharp teeth through skin and sinew. Blood oozes into my mouth. As I kill her, I sob.

Why did she suck the soul of me from the wounds she made? Why am I wolf because of her? Or did it always lurk there, needing only the pain she made to release the ferocity?

But she is dead.

I had forgotten. I had sought her in this pleasant town.

Ah, now the other is dead, too.

Let murder drown me until I am nothing but a snarling speck, harmless and protected by my infinitesimal size.

Oh, God, my bloody darling . . .

Consuming Passion

I travel swiftly and cautiously over the soft, dry wood-shavings. All around me loom the canvas-covered piles of timber. It is on nights as dark as this that I enjoy my work; the fruits of my labours are that much more apparent.

I feel my mouth go dry, as dry as the wood I tread on; my breath comes quickly, in and out of my lungs; my heart pounds heavily against my ribs. Here is a place, a dark, quiet place with light dowelling stacked high. Fine kindling.

From my special little pocket, I extract my shiny petrol lighter. Press of a thumb, scrape of a wheel, a random spark shoots from flint to wick—and lights the invisible fumes. How perfect it is, this little pointed, flickering flame.

In my jacket pockets is paper, screwed up tight. I stuff it into gaps between the heaped dowels. Now I apply the flame.

Beautifully, the fire begins to lick explorative tongues delicately upwards, darting along the wood, further and further. The delicious smell of woodsmoke fills my lungs.

I stand back and I want to laugh at the flaming glory I have created. It will soon engulf the stacks of timber, but now I must run away. Far away. To be found here would mean that my days of creation would be over. It is warm, near the fire, and the night air chills me as I run.

Another Big Blaze
ARSON STRONGLY SUSPECTED
Is maniac at large?

Jordan Mennell reads the headline with a slightly thumping heart. A faint smile plays around his well-shaped mouth. His eyes, too bright for grey eyes, scan the columns avidly.

Once more a masterpiece accomplished.

This makes ten. Ten great works of heart. Ten triumphs; ten little note-books with ten collections of clippings pasted neatly in them. And they have a name for him now.

Pyro Jack!

His pseudonym.

Tomorrow I try for eleven. No more petty ignitions of garden bonfires; no more the occasional surreptitiously dropped match in a waste-paper bin. Big ones from now on. Vast timber yards, rubber dumps, petrol reservoirs. Like God I create the flame which destroys. Yes, I am a creator and a destroyer. The power is in my hands. The glory of leaping, yelling, roaring, soaring flames—the red, yellow and blue, the gold and the silver. The tall columns of smoke and the red glow on the skyline. And frantic, terrified little men hopping about, impotent and frightened.

Tomorrow, the eleventh and greatest ever creation. Tomorrow—Dennissen's the furniture store. No watchman; quite safe. Eight storeys of combustibles. A fitting monument to my power. Today, dull wood and fabric; lifeless. Tomorrow—a glorious, sentient mountain.

He pulls on the black trousers, the dark shirt, the soft-soled shoes; feels for the lighter, checks for paper. Paper safe and crinkly against his thigh; lighter hard and smooth.

He goes out of the brown and grubby back door from which the paint is peeling. He turns the rusty key in the stiff lock; picks a silent path through the rubble of the yard, past the dilapidated shed with the door which hangs on one hinge. Over the leaning fence and into the narrow, cindered alley.

Softly, he crunches along, keeping to the maze of alleyways which run between the identical banks of houses. Bright lights of the High Street before him. A sudden dash across it into the gloom of another narrow alley. But this one is of firm concrete, a wall on one side, a tall corrugated-iron fence on the other. The fence is pointed at the top, like triangular fingers clutching for the sky.

Panting now, after the exertion of the swift run across the deserted main street. A white-painted sign, white foam on the undulating sea of the corrugated fence. He removes his jacket.

With a quick movement, he sends the jacket sailing upwards so that it falls and hangs on the barbs of the fence. An agile jump and his hands are on the top of the fence, padded by his jacket. With little obvious effort, he hauls himself carefully over the fence and, hanging for a moment by one hand, grasps his jacket with the other and drops. The jacket comes with him, but it rips loudly as it comes. He puts it on again and looks around him.

He can guess what the dark silhouettes are; old chests of drawers, ancient divans, bed-springs.

Now he takes out his sharp, steel knife and begins to force the lock on the door. He hacks at the wood which surrounds the lock and knows that this damage may be discovered. Good, he thinks, they will know that I am responsible.

I am in a dark passage full of the odours of wood-polish and veneer and cloth. I walk along the passage and find the stairway which leads down into the basement. I have been here before. I bought a chair in the second-hand department. That department is in the basement.

I know what I must do. I must ignite the furniture in the basement, then I must go quickly up to the eighth floor and light the fabrics they keep there. Then I must open some windows so that a breeze will fan the flames.

I take out my small pocket-torch and flash it around the basement. A carpet on the floor, wardrobes, tallboys, bookcases. Many of them frail-looking. All the better. A cupboard painted dull cream and very flimsy. The ideal spot. I take the paper from my pocket and put it along the bottom shelf of the cupboard. Some curtains partition off another piece of the department. I walk over to them and rip them down; they tear with a tiny tinkle of curtain rings.

Stuffing the curtains into other shelves of the cupboard, I take out my lighter. A great feeling of elation and power begins to surge through my body. I breathe heavily, my hand shakes a little, my heart is beating a frenzied tattoo against my rib-cage. This is the ultimate of sensations, almost all I desire. I press my thumb on the lighter.

Nothing happens, a brief spark but that is all. I press it again, there is a tiny snap. I know that sound, the sound when the flint is finished. I moan in anguish and pass my hands through my hair in violent frustration. I glare with rage at the cupboard. And the cupboard bursts into flames.

Not with a delicate flicker of light, but with a sudden snap and a roar and it is burning; burning so brightly.

I stare at a cabinet and will it to burn. But nothing happens. Then I realize that the flames are licking nearer to me. I turn and run from the basement, up the stairs, three at a time, opening windows at every landing. Up another flight of stairs, and another, and another, until I am breathing very heavily and irregularly and I am at the top of the building.

But I realize I have no matches, no lighter, nothing with which to create another blaze. I feel frustrated among the rolls of cloth, the cotton and the nylon which will burn so well. I feel like a writer without a pen, an artist without his brushes. The canvas is before me, but I have nothing with which to paint it, to turn it into glowing beauty.

Anger once more consumes me. Is God so frustrated when He works *His* miracles? I wish with all my heart that the cotton and the nylon will burn. And it does. It begins to burn all around me, quite suddenly. I stand for a long moment and revel in the passionate wonder of the dancing flames. I breathe in the smell of the burning fabric.

Then I realize that if I stay and watch, I will no longer be alive. No longer will I be able to create more grandeur and magnificence. I turn and dash down the stairs. As I reach the last flight, I see a glow, a glorious glow, in the basement.

I fling open the door through which I entered and rush out into the yard. The fence stops me. Why hadn't I thought about the fence before? Leering, jeering fence! My teeth clench tightly, twisting my mouth. I sob in anger. And the fence begins to melt. A hole appears in it; drops of white-hot metal fall from the edges of the hole. I dash through, howling as a piece of molten iron drops on my shoulder and sets my jacket ablaze. I tear off the garment and fling it behind me as I run down the alley the way I came. No one is in the High Street. I run across the road into the safety of the alley-ways behind the rows of houses. I moan softly to myself; the pain in my shoulder is agonizing.

Jordan Mennell sits in the shabby armchair reading his paper. He is dressed only in a pair of pyjama trousers and his right shoulder is crudely smothered in a large piece of medical plaster which is wrinkled and dirty.

The same faint smile is on his face, the same bright light in his eyes. He is reading his latest reviews.

One of the most disastrous fires in South London!
WHO IS PYRO JACK?

says one critic. Praise indeed! The critic mentions that the police suspect arson once more. And Pyro Jack, as the public knows Jordan Mennell, is credited. The eleventh big fire in the area within two weeks. Jordan Mennell has been able to see the flames from his bedroom window. He decides that this was the biggest. His unnamed critic agrees. And now Jordan Mennell has the power to create more great fires wherever he pleases. If his anger is sufficiently roused, he supposes, he can start a blaze anywhere he wishes. He is content.

The pain in his shoulder is great, but it will go away soon. His eyes follow the front-page columns, reading the speculations and assertions. He comes to a paragraph and the smile clears from his mouth as it opens slightly. The police have a clue. A charred jacket which was left on the scene of the fire.

For a moment, Jordan Mennell knows concern. But then he is his old self, his old powerful self. With his new talents, he can defy the police even though they may catch him. He knows what he is capable of, now. Concentration will help him channel his talent, he will not need to feel anger, there will be other emotions. Concentration and power. He has both.

I am dressing, ready to go to work, when there comes a terse knocking on the door of my house. I am puzzled but I finish dressing before I walk down the narrow stairs which creak, and reach out my hand to the handle of the door. As I turn it, I have an inkling of who my caller is. I open the door slowly and confront the man who stands on my step, his left foot close to a bottle of milk and a carton of eggs; his right foot on the cracked concrete of my path. His trousers are black, like his shoes; his raincoat is khaki and grubby. He wears a dark jacket, a striped shirt and a blue tie. He has a double chin and a small moustache and his eyes are deep blue under thick eyebrows. On top of his head is a brown felt trilby. He is, I feel certain, a plainclothes policeman.

"Yes?" I enquire, shortly.

"Mr. Jordan Mennell?" He knows who I am but I answer him all the same.

"Yes," I tell him. I know the next words before he speaks them.

"I am a police officer. I wonder if I might come in and ask you a few questions?" His voice is gruff and he attempts a politeness which is not in his nature; there is a rock core beneath this very thin veneer.

What else can I say but "Very well."

He enters and I lead him into my small sitting-room. I indicate a chair and the movement sends spasms of pain through my throbbing shoulder. I manage to smile.

"What can I do for you, officer? Looking for burglars?"

"No, sir," this he says slowly. "It's about the big fire at Dennissen's."

"I read about it this morning," I say, keeping perfect control of myself. "A terrible catastrophe."

"Yes, sir. The whole place was gutted. Your jacket was found nearby." This is an attempt to shock me. A bluff. But I am ready for this policeman with his shallow cunning.

"My jacket!" I manage to seem astounded. "But that is impossible!"

"Your name was on a tag fixed inside the jacket, sir. Most of the right side of the jacket was burned, but much of it was left when we found it. Perhaps you would like to come along to the station and identify the jacket, sir?"

I feel anger coursing inside me, but I control my emotion and smile again. "Very well, officer, but I am sure you are mistaken." What can they do to me, anyway? I am invincible.

We reach the red-brick police-station and walk together along a cold marble passage, up a short flight of stairs and into a warm room. There is a gas-fire burning against one wall. The desk has wire trays and papers on it—and a parcel. There is a small window which looks out on to the street. A grey street, with an occasional dull-coloured car flashing by, or a darkly-dressed man. These people should feel honoured that I bring such magnificent colour into their lives. But instead they resent me. It is wrong, but I must accept it.

The policeman walks over to the desk after shutting the door behind us. He unwraps the parcel and discloses the remains of the coat I wore last night.

I feel annoyed because I have been so careless. I had assumed that the jacket would have burned to ashes.

I feel another upsurge of power within me, just as a uniformed policeman enters. He begins to tidy up the desk.

"That is my coat," I say, after having glanced at it.

"And," I add grandly, "I was responsible for all eleven fires you have been worrying about. I shall also be the cause of many more."

"Pyro Jack, my God!" says the younger uniformed policeman. I bow slightly to him as he makes for the door with an armful of papers, bent on telling the news to his companions no doubt. After all, I am a personality whose work has been very much in the public eye recently. They may ask me for my autograph. I shall refuse.

However, I am still angry, but manage to retain a mask of calm.

The policeman is visibly shocked by my statement, but he recovers his composure enough to say "In which case, Mr Mennell, perhaps you'd like to make a statement."

"I have made all the statement I wish to make," I reply, "Now I must leave."

"Oh, no you don't!" He moves forward to stop me as I make for the door.

I wheel around and glare at him, if only he would burn too, it would be easier for me.

He shrieks horribly as the flames lick at his flesh. But he has stopped by the time I reach the entrance of the police station.

"*Stop him!* That's Pyro Jack!" The young policeman yells shrilly, excitedly. Another policeman, entering the front of the building, moves forward to stop me. I burn his uniform. He begins to beat frantically at the flames.

I walk calmly out of the place and stroll along the street. A few minutes later, a police-car pulls up beside the pavement. I melt it.

The men inside scream in terror.

I laugh out loud, glorying in my magnificent power. The instinct of self-preservation is a wonderful thing.

People rushing. People shouting. People pushing. People grasping. People burning brightly like giant skipping fireflies, a glorious dance of death.

I walk on down the long brick-lined avenues. I stride along burning and melting anyone or anything which comes in my way. I can conquer the world, and turn it into leaping flames, like a second sun. It shall burn in the heavens as it did millions of years ago.

I thrill jubilantly and my steps are light and buoyant. An hour passes, then manlike, mis-shapen things shuffle clumsily towards me. They have a single broad eye and carry guns in thick-fingered hands.

"Stop, Mennell! Stop, or we shoot!"

Asbestos! Of course, I see it now, I cannot burn asbestos. And those guns can kill me. I shudder and wish that guns would catch fire, too. They melt.

But the men in the asbestos suits draw nearer. They reach out their coarse, ungainly hands to grasp me.

I draw back, the indignity of it all appals me. I run away from them towards a tall building; a tall white building. The public library.

A woman shrieks as I rush inside, but I ignore her and run on. The clumping of my pursuers' boots echoes down the corridor towards me. I dash into a high-roofed room lined with bookshelves.

The men come nearer and nearer, I stare wildly around me, looking for a route of escape—but I have entered through the only door. Framed in it now are the three asbestos-clad monsters.

It is unfair. They should herald me as master of the world, not treat me as if I were an abnormal beast. I am a supernormal man!

They spread out their arms and move in a cautious semicircle towards me. I feel enraged at myself and admit that my own blind folly has led me to this trap.

"Back! Get back!" I roar, my voice reverberating round the lofty room. "Back, or I will destroy you!" Still they come nearer, light glinting on their cyclops' eyes, their faceplates.

I scream at them, but the fools still advance. I deserve to burn myself, for my negligence. A flicker of flame appears on my trousers, runs sensuously up my leg, caresses my thigh. Frantically, I attempt to beat it out, but it is too late. I can start fires but cannot extinguish them—I have never wanted to.

I glare at the books. Voltaire, Dickens, Dostoevsky, Shakespeare, Conrad, Hemingway surround me, glaring back, mocking me. Their work will last, they seem to say. Mine is finished.

My anger sets tongues of orange flames writhing around the

books. Everywhere on the shelves the books began to burn. I feel the heat of my flaming clothes, the pain of the fire. Softly, at first, I begin to laugh. I have achieved some small measure of triumph.

The Ruins

Maldoon picked his way over the ruins, his sombre face speckled with gleaming drops of sweat as if he had covered it with jewels.

The ruins went away from him in all directions beneath the blue and glowing sky, spikes of masonry, jumbled concrete, pools of ash, so that the whole bleak landscape took on the aspect of sea-carved rocks at low tide. The sun shone and the ruins lay peacefully beneath; pale shadows having nothing ominous or mysterious about them. Maldoon felt safe in the ruins.

He took off his jacket and sat on a slab of concrete from which protruded rusted wires, curling back on themselves like a sculpture depicting space and time. In fact the ruins were that—a mighty sculpture, a monument created by the random and ambivalent machinations of mankind—a monument to time and space and to the sacrifices men had made to understand it. Maldoon realized his thoughts were rambling. He lit a cigarette and drank some water from his flask.

He had been travelling over the ruins for a long time, searching for signs of life but finding nothing. He was regretting the notion that had sent him into the ruins. There were no signs of the previous explorers who had not returned; no mark scratched on stone, no note, no shred of cloth, no skeleton. The ruins were barren.

Maldoon stood up, putting his flask away and dropping his cigarette into a crevice. He stared ahead of him at the jagged horizon, turned his body round. The strange thing was that his view to the horizon was never interrupted. No crumpled building or collapsing wall ever blocked his vision. The horizon was on all sides, giving him the peculiar sensation of standing in the centre of a huge disc which drifted in an infinity of blue sky.

He frowned. The sun was directly overhead and he had no idea which direction he had come from. Now that he considered it, he couldn't remember the sun changing its position or, for that matter, night ever falling. Hadn't the light always been so? Yet he thought he had been travelling for several days.

Slowly he began to make his way across the ruins again, stumbling sometimes, half-falling, jumping from slab of masonry to pile of broken bricks, leaning against the shattered wall of a house with one hand as he inched his way around the ash-pools which he mistrusted, though there was no cause for his wariness as he remembered.

At length, something close to panic began to fill him and he wished very strongly that he had not come to the ruins, wished that he was back amongst people again, amidst orderly streets of neat houses and solid, well-filled shops. He looked about him hopefully and, as if his wish had been answered by some magical spirit, he saw on the horizon a line of tall, complete-looking buildings which might possibly be part of a town.

His speed increased; his progress was no longer such hard going.

And, he noted, laughing at himself for his earlier fancies, the sun was beginning to set. With luck he could make the town before night.

He began to leap from point to point, but he had misjudged his distance from the town and night came while he was still about a mile away. But he was heartened further by the sight of the lights shining out of the buildings. Perhaps this was even the town he had left? One town was much like another, seen from the distance. With the lights to guide him he was soon at the town's outskirts. Here the streets were deserted, though illuminated by splendid lamps, and he guessed that the inhabitants had gone to bed. Getting closer to the city-centre, he heard traffic noises and saw cars moving through the streets, people on the boulevards, cafés open for business.

He ignored the notion that there was something incomplete about the city. He was tired and was seeing things in a peculiar perspective. Also the hot sun of the day might well have given him sunstroke.

The city was new to him, though familiar enough in its general layout. It was, like most cities he knew, planned around a central square with the main streets radiating from the square like the spokes from a wheel, with an outer circle of suburbs.

Maldoon entered a café and ordered a meal. The proprietor was an old man with a gnomish face and a deferential manner. He put the plate of food before Maldoon, averting his eyes. Maldoon began to eat.

Presently a girl came into the café, glanced around at the few available seats and chose one opposite Maldoon. "Is this seat taken?" she asked him.

He waved his fork and shook his head, his mouth too full for speech.

She smiled and sat down daintily. She picked up the menu and studied it, giving her order to the proprietor who received it with a little bow and hurried back to the kitchen.

"It's a beautiful night for the time of the year," Maldoon said, "isn't it?"

"Ah, yes . . ." She appeared to be confused.

"I'm sorry," he said. "I hope you don't think I'm . . ."

"No, no."

"I have just come in from the ruins," he told her. "I was doing a bit of exploring. They stretch for miles and miles. Sometimes I think they must cover the planet. Does anyone know?"

She laughed. "You look tired—hadn't you better get some sleep?"

"I'm a stranger here. Can you recommend an hotel?"

"Not really. Being a resident, as it were, I don't know much about the hotels. There's one up the road, though, that looks all right."

"I'll try that, then."

Her meal was brought to her. She thanked the proprietor with a quick smile. He saw that she had ordered the same meal.

He let her eat without interruption. Now that he was seated, his body felt numb with tiredness. He looked forward to a good night's sleep.

The girl got up. She looked at him with curiosity. "I'd bet-

ter show you where that hotel is." She smiled sympatheti-
cally.

"Oh, thanks." He got up and left the café with her. As
they walked along the street he thought of something.
Shouldn't he have paid for his meal? He couldn't remember.
But the owner of the café wouldn't have let him walk out
like that, anyway, so it must be all right.

He walked along beside the girl, his shoulders feeling as if
they were carrying a tremendous weight, his muscles aching
and his legs weak.

How had he managed to cross such a huge area of the ruins? Surely he hadn't walked all that way? What way? How
much way? Where way?

"Are you sure you can make it?" said the girl distinctly,
her lips close to his ear. She spoke as if repeating herself.

"Yes."

"Well come on, it's not much further."

He followed her, but now he was crawling. He heard a
voice that was not his own crying: "Can somebody give me a
hand?"

He lay on the uneven surface of the ruins and the sun was
directly over his head. He turned and saw the horizon in the
far distance; he turned his eyes in the other direction and
there, too, were ruins stretching to the horizon. He felt like a
giant spread-eagled and crucified on the ruins. As he pushed
himself into a sitting position, his body seemed to diminish
until he was normal size again.

Normal size? What was normal size? What yardstick had
he with which to measure the ruins? They were of all sizes,
all shapes. Yet not one of them, however high, blocked his
view of the horizon.

He had lost his jacket and his cigarettes. He stood up un-
steadily and stared around him.

Was he some kind of outcast? He couldn't remember. There
had to be some reason for his being here. Someone had put
him here. People from the city had taken the trouble to
transport him here.

Or had they? And if they had, *why* had they?

The problem did not concern him for very long. He began
to move over the ruins once again, pausing sometimes to in-

spect a building that seemed to have been sliced down the centre, leaving its floors intact and exposed like those of a doll's house. Yet he could find no clue to answer any of the questions which drifted and dispersed in his mind.

By now, he had forgotten about the city, even; had forgotten that he had had a jacket, that he had smoked cigarettes, felt no need for either.

Later, he sat down on a pile of broken tiles and looked around him. To his left a tower leaned. Though it seemed that something had crushed it from two angles, it still stood upright. His logic told him it should have fallen, yet the tower was frozen there. He stopped looking at it, but too late to stop the rising sensation of fear which the sight created.

He got up and walked carefully away from the tower, not looking back, and then broke into a stumbling run.

But he saw that all the buildings seemed about to fall, all the towers and houses and columns were pitched at an angle which said that they *must* fall.

Why hadn't he noticed it before? What was wrong?

With the fear, his knowledge of his identity began to re-emerge.

He remembered his name and a little of the past as far back as his visit to the city. Then he remembered his days-long journey over the ruins, beneath a sun that did not set, a sky that did not change, seeing on all sides the horizon which *should* have been obscured by the great piles of ruined architecture and yet was *not*.

He stopped, shaking with hatred of the ruins, striving to bring back a memory of *before* the ruins, but he could not.

What was this? Dream? Drug-vision? Madness? Surely there was something more than the ruins? Had the city been just an illusion?

He closed his eyes, his body tottering. In the darkness which came with the closing of his eyes, he said to himself: *Well, Maldoon, do you still insist on continuing this experiment? Do you still wish to abolish identity and time and space as illusion-creating illusions?*

And he called back to himself, aloud:

"What do you mean? What do you *mean?*"

And he opened his eyes again and there were the bright ruins, sharp beneath the great, pale sun in the blue sky.

(Sun, sky, ruins + Maldoon = Maldoon—Maldoon.)

Now, slowly, he began to calm, his questions and his memories, for what they were worth, drifting apart.

He steadied himself on the ruins and walked towards a particularly large ash-pool. He stopped when he reached it. He stared down into it. He put his fingers to his lips and mused over the ash-pool.

He picked up a piece of brick and flung it down into the grey ash. When it reached the surface, the brick disappeared without disturbing the ash.

He took another brick and another and hurled them down. The same thing happened. The same thing didn't happen.

A shadow fell across him. He looked up and saw a tall building rising above him. It consisted of a huge shaft built of glass bricks with a series of platforms going up and up until at the top there was the last platform with a dome over it. A man stood there, beckoning to him.

He ran towards the tower, found he could spring on to the first platform and from that one to the next until he reached the platform covered by the dome.

A man similar to a frog was waiting for him.

"Look down there, Maldoon," he said.

Maldoon looked out over the neat city spread below. Each block was of exactly the same dimensions, each one was square.

The man waved his reptilian hand. The light shone through it, grey as the ash.

"A country is like a woman," said the man. "Look down there. It *wants* to be subdued, wants to be bested by a strong man. I did it. I quieted the country's perturbation—and raped it!"

The frog-man looked self-satisfied.

"It's peaceful," said Maldoon.

"The most peaceful country in the system," the man-frog quipped. "The most peaceful system in the country. Who are you, Maldoon?"

"Either you or me," said Maldoon, forgetting his name.

"Jump, Maldoon," said the man similar to a frog.

Maldoon merely stood there.

"Jump!"

He began to clamber around the ash-pool.

(Sun, sky, ruins + Maldoon) = (Maldoon—Maldoon)

His name was a throb in his head, merely a throb in his head. Mal-*doon*, Mal-*doon*, Mal-*doon*.

Had it ever been his name? Perhaps not. Perhaps it had always been—mal-*doon*, mal-*doon*—merely a throb in his head.

Yet, apart from the ruins and the light, there was nothing else to know.

He paused. Was that a memory? That, at the back there?

Out—mal-doon, mal-doon—out—maldoon—concentrate, mal-doon.

The ruins appeared to blur for a moment and he stared at them sharply, suspiciously. They seemed to be folding themselves around him. No, he was folding himself around them. He flowed around them, over them, through them.

Maldoon! The cry from somewhere was imperious, desperate, ironic.

Yes, he thought, *which way?*

All or nothing, Maldoon, he cried to himself, *nothing or nothing, all or all!*

Out here is in here and it is infinite. He remembered, or was told, he could not tell.

(Infinity + Maldoon) = (Infinity)

With relief, he was glad to be back. Things were right again. He paused and sat on a piece of broken concrete which sprouted spliced hawsers and which changed to a mound of soft soil with reeds growing from it. Below him was the city—roofs, chimneys, church-spires, parks, cinemas, smoke drifting. Familiar, yet not what he wanted.

He got up from the mound and began to walk down the path towards the city, still only half-aware of who he was, why he was, what he was and how he was.

"Why do I tire myself out trying," he thought. "One day I shan't be able to exert enough will to pull myself back and they'll find me up here either raving or curled up in a neat little bundle."

Yet he could not decide, still, which was true—the city below or the ruins.

"Are they both real?" he thought as he walked off the grass and on to the road leading into the city.

He sauntered along the road, passing under a railway bridge of thick girders and peeling green paint, turned a corner into a side-street which was full of the smoky smell of autumn. The houses were of red-brick and terraced with tiny gardens submerged beneath huge, overgrown hedges. Behind one of the hedges he heard children playing. He stopped and put his head round the hedge, watching them with their coloured bricks, building and pushing them down again.

When one of the children noticed him and looked up, he pulled his head back and walked on along the street.

But he was not to escape with impunity. The child cried "It's him!" and followed him along the street with its companions chorusing rhythmically: "Mad Maldoon! Mad Maldoon! Mad Maldoon—he's a loon!" and laughing at this old jest.

He pretended not to notice them.

They only followed him to the end of the street and he was grateful for this, at least. It was getting late. Dusk was falling over the houses. His footfalls echoed among the roofs, clattering hollowly from chimney pot to chimney pot.

Mad Maldoon, mad maldoon, madmaldoonmaldoonmaldoon.

Heart-beats joined in, maldoon, maldoon, head-beats, maldoon, maldoon and the houses were still there but superimposed on the ruins, the echoes swimming amongst their unreal chimney pots.

The dusk gave way to night, the night to light and slowly the houses vanished.

The bright ruins stretched away, never obscuring his view of the horizon. The blue, blue sky was above, and the sun which did not change its position.

The ash-pools, he avoided. The tumbling ruins, fixed and frozen in time and space, did not fall.

What caused the ruins?

He had completely forgotten.

There were just the ruins now, as the sky and the sun went out but the light remained. Just the sound of some unseen surf pounding at the last vestiges of his identity.

Mal-doon, mal-doon, mal-doon.

Ruins past, ruins present, ruins future.

He absorbed the ruins and they him. He and they went away for ever, for now there was no horizon.

The mind could clothe the ruins, but now there was no mind.

Soon, there were no ruins.

The Pleasure Garden
of Felipe Sagittarius

The air was still and warm, the sun bright and the sky blue
above the ruins of Berlin as I clambered over piles of weed-
covered brick and broken concrete on my way to investigate
the murder of an unknown man in the garden of Police Chief
Bismarck.

My name is Minos Aquilinas, top Metatemporal Investigator of Europe, and this job was going to be a tough one, I
knew.

Don't ask me the location or the date. I never bother to
find out things like that, they only confuse me. With me it's
instinct, win or lose.

They'd given me all the information there was. The dead
man had already had an autopsy. Nothing unusual about him
except that he had paper lungs—disposable lungs. That
pinned him down a little. The only place I knew of where
they still used paper lungs was Rome. What was a Roman
doing in Berlin? Why was he murdered in Police Chief
Bismarck's garden? He'd been strangled, that I'd been told. It
wasn't hard to strangle a man with paper lungs, it didn't take
long. But who and why were harder questions to answer
right then.

It was a long way across the ruins to Bismarck's place.
Rubble stretched in all directions and only here and there
could you see a landmark—what was left of the Reichstag,
the Brandenburg Gate, the Brechtsmuseum and a few other
places like that.

I stopped to lean on the only remaining wall of a house,

147

took off my jacket and loosened my tie, wiped my forehead and neck with my handkerchief and lit a cheroot. The wall gave me some shade and I felt a little cooler by the time I was ready to press on.

As I mounted a big heap of brick on which a lot of blue weeds grew I saw the Bismarck place ahead. Built of heavy, black-veined, marble, in the kind of Valhalla/Olympus mixture they went in for, it was fronted by a smooth, green lawn and backed by a garden that was surrounded by such a high wall I only glimpsed the leaves of some of the foliage even though I was looking down on the place. The thick Grecian columns flanking the porch were topped by a baroque façade covered in bas-reliefs showing men in horned helmets killing dragons and one another apparently indiscriminately.

I picked my way down to the lawn and walked across it, then up some steps until I'd crossed to the front door. It was big and heavy, bronze I guessed, with more bas-reliefs, this time of clean-shaven characters in more ornate and complicated armour with two-handed swords and riding horses. Some had lances and axes. I pulled the bell and waited.

I had plenty of time to study the pictures before one of the doors swung open and an old man in a semi-military suit, holding himself straight by an effort, raised a white eyebrow at me.

I told him my name and he let me in to a cool, dark hall full of the same kinds of armour the men on the door had been wearing. He opened a door on the right and told me to wait. The room I was in was all iron and leather—weapons on the walls and leather-covered furniture on the carpet.

Thick velvet curtains were drawn back from the window and I stood looking out over the quiet ruins, smoked another stick, popped the butt in a green pot and put my jacket back on.

The old man came in again and I followed him out of that room, along the hall, up one flight of the wide stairs and in to a huge, less cluttered room where I found the guy I'd come to see.

He stood in the middle of the carpet. He was wearing a heavily ornamented helmet with a spike on the top, a deep blue uniform covered in badges, gold and black epaulettes, shiny jackboots and steel spurs. He looked about seventy and very tough. He had bushy grey eyebrows and a big, carefully combed moustache. As I came in he grunted and one arm sprang into a horizontal position, pointing at me.

"Herr Aquilinas. I am Otto von Bismarck, Chief of Berlin's police."

I shook the hand. Actually it shook me, all over.

"Quite a turn up," I said. "A murder in the garden of the man who's supposed to prevent murders."

His face must have been paralysed or something because it didn't move except when he spoke, and even then it didn't move much.

"Quite so," he said. "We were reluctant to call you in, of course. But I think this is your specialty."

"Maybe. Is the body still here?"

"In the kitchen. The autopsy was performed here. Paper lungs—you know about that?"

"I know. Now, if I've got it right, you heard nothing in the night—"

"Oh, yes, I did hear something—the barking of my wolf-hounds. One of the servants investigated but found nothing."

"What time was this?"

"Time?"

"What did the clock say?"

"About two in the morning."

"When was the body found?"

"About ten—the gardener discovered it in the vine grove."

"Right—let's look at the body and then talk to the gardener."

He took me to the kitchen. One of the windows was opened on to a lush garden, full of tall, brightly coloured shrubs of every possible shade. An intoxicating scent came from the garden. It made me feel randy. I turned to look at the corpse lying on a scrubbed deal table covered in a sheet.

I pulled back the sheet. The body was naked. It looked old but strong, deeply tanned. The head was big and its most noticeable feature was the heavy black moustache. The body wasn't what it had been. First there were the marks of strangulation around the throat, as well as swelling on wrists, forearms and legs which seemed to indicate that the victim had also been tied up recently. The whole of the front of the torso had been opened for the autopsy and whoever had stitched it up again hadn't been too careful.

"What about clothes?" I asked the Police Chief.

Bismarck shook his head and pointed to a chair standing beside the table. "That was all we found."

There was a pair of neatly folded paper lungs, a bit the worse for wear. The trouble with disposable lungs was that while you never had to worry about smoking or any of the other causes of lung disease, the lungs had to be changed regularly. This was expensive, particularly in Rome where there was no State-controlled Lung Service as there had been in most of the European City-States until a few years before the war when the longer-lasting polythene lung had superseded the paper one. There was also a wrist-watch and a pair of red shoes with long, curling toes.

I picked up one of the shoes. Middle Eastern workmanship. I looked at the watch. It was heavy, old, tarnished and Russian. The strap was new, pigskin, with "Made in England" stamped on it.

"I see why they called us," I said.

"There *were* certain anachronisms," Bismarck admitted.

"This gardener who found him, can I talk to him?"

Bismarck went to the window and called: "Felipe!"

The foliage seemed to fold back of its own volition and a dark haired young man came through it. He was tall, long-faced and pale. He held an elegant watering can in one hand. He was dressed in a dark-green high-collared shirt and matching trousers.

We looked at one another through the window.

"This is my gardener, Felipe Sagittarius," Bismarck said.

Sagittarius bowed, his eyes amused. Bismarck didn't seem to notice.

"Can you let me see where you found the body?" I asked.

"Sure," said Sagittarius.

"I shall wait here," Bismarck told me as I went towards the kitchen door.

"Okay." I stepped into the garden and let Sagittarius show me the way. Once again the shrubs seemed to part on their own.

The scent was still thick and erotic. Most of the plants had dark, fleshy leaves and flowers of deep reds, purples and blues. Here and there were clusters of heavy yellow and pink.

The grass I was walking on seemed to crawl under my feet and the weird shapes of the trunks and stems of the shrubs didn't make me feel like taking a snooze in that garden.

"This is all your work is it, Sagittarius?" I asked.

He nodded and kept walking.

"Original," I said. "Never seen one like it before."

Sagittarius turned then and pointed a thumb behind him. "This is the place."

We were standing in a little glade almost entirely surrounded by thick vines that curled about their trellises like snakes. On the far side of the glade I could see where some of the vines had been ripped and the trellis torn and I guessed there had been a fight. I still couldn't work out why the victim had been untied before the murderer strangled him—it must have been before, or else there wouldn't have been a fight. I checked the scene, but there were no clues. Through the place where the trellis was torn I saw a small summerhouse, built to represent a Chinese pavilion, all red, yellow and black lacquer with highlights picked out in gold. It didn't fit with the architecture of the house.

"What's that?" I asked the gardener.

"Nothing," he said sulkily, evidently sorry I'd seen it.

"I'll take a look at it anyway."

He shrugged but didn't offer to lead on. I moved between the trellises until I reached the pavilion. Sagittarius followed slowly. I took the short flight of wooden steps up to the veranda and tried the door. It opened. I walked in. There seemed to be only one room, a bedroom. The bed needed making and it looked as if two people had left it in a hurry. There was a pair of nylons tucked half under the pillow and a pair of man's underpants on the floor. The sheets were very white, the furnishings very oriental and rich.

Sagittarius was standing in the doorway.

"Your place?" I said.

"No." He sounded offended. "The Police Chief's."

I grinned.

Sagittarius burst into rhapsody. "The languorous scents, the very menace of the plants, the *heaviness* in the air of the garden, must surely stir the blood of even the most ancient man. This is the only place he can relax. That is what I'm employed for—why he gives me my head."

"Has this," I said, pointing to the bed, "anything to do with last night?"

"He was probably here when it happened, but I . . ." Sagittarius shook his head and I wondered if there was anything he'd meant to imply which I'd missed.

I saw something on the floor, stooped and picked it up. A pendant with the initials E.B. engraved on it in Gothic script.

"Who's E.B.?" I said.

"Only the garden interests me, Mr. Aquilinas—I do not know who she is."

I looked out at the weird garden. "Why does it interest you—what's all this for? You're not doing it to his orders, are you? You're doing it for yourself."

Sagittarius smiled bleakly. "You are astute." He waved an arm at the warm foliage that seemed more reptilian than plant and more mammalian, in its own way, than either. "You know what I see out there? I see deep-sea canyons where lost submarines cruise through a silence of twilit green, threatened by the waving tentacles of predators, half-fish, half-plant, and watched by the eyes of long-dead mermen whose blood went to feed their young; where squids and rays fight in a graceful dance of death, clouds of black ink merging with clouds of red blood, drifting to the surface, sipped at by sharks in passing, where they will be seen by mariners leaning over the rails of their ships; maddened, the mariners will fling themselves overboard to sail slowly towards those distant plant-creatures already feasting on the corpse of squid and ray. This is the world I can bring to the land—that is my ambition."

He stared at me, paused, and said: "My skull—*it's like a monstrous gold-fish bowl!*"

I nipped back to the house to find Bismarck had returned to his room. He was sitting in a plush armchair, a hidden HiFi playing, of all things, a Ravel String Quartet.

"No Wagner?" I said and then: "Who's E.B.?"

"Later," he said. "My assistant will answer your questions for the moment. He should be waiting for you outside."

There was a car parked outside the house—a battered Volkswagen containing a neatly uniformed man of below average height, a small tooth-brush moustache, a stray lock of black hair falling over his forehead, black gloves on his hands which gripped a military cane in his lap. When he saw me come out he smiled, said, "Aha," and got briskly from the car to shake my hand with a slight bow.

"Adolf Hitler," he said. "Captain of Uniformed Detectives in Precinct XII. Police Chief Bismarck has put me at your service."

"Glad to hear it. Do you know much about him?"

Hitler opened the car door for me and I got in. He went round the other side, slid into the driving seat.

"The chief?" He shook his head. "He is somewhat remote. I do not know him well—there are several ranks between us. Usually my orders come from him indirectly. This time he chose to see me himself and give me my orders."

"What were they, these orders?"

"Simply to help you in this investigation."

"There isn't much to investigate. You're completely loyal to your chief I take it?"

"Of course." Hitler seemed honestly puzzled. He started the car and we drove down the drive and out along a flat, white road, surmounted on both sides by great heaps of overgrown rubble.

"The murdered man had paper lungs, eh?" he said.

"Yes. Guess he must have come from Rome. He looked a bit like an Italian."

"Or a Jew, eh?"

"I don't think so. What made you think that?"

"The Russian watch, the Oriental shoes—the nose. That was a big nose he had. And they still have paper lungs in Moscow, you know."

His logic seemed a bit off-beat to me but I let it pass. We turned a corner and entered a residential section where a lot of buildings were still standing. I noticed that one of them had a bar in its cellar. "How about a drink?" I said.

"Here?" He seemed surprised, or maybe nervous.

"Why not?"

So he stopped the car and we went down the steps into the bar. A girl was singing. She was a plumpish brunette with a small, good voice. She was singing in English and I caught the chorus:

> "Nobody's grievin' for Steven,
>   And Stevie ain't grievin' no more,
>   For Steve took his life in a prison cell,
>   And Johnny took a new whore."

It was the latest hit in England. We ordered beers from the bartender. He seemed to know Hitler well because he laughed and slapped him on the shoulder and didn't charge us for the beer. Hitler seemed embarrassed.

"Who was that?" I asked.

"Oh, his name is Weill. I know him slightly."

"More than slightly, it looks like."

Hitler seemed unhappy and undid his uniform jacket, tilted his cap back on his head and tried unsuccessfully to push back the stray lock of hair. He looked a sad little man and I felt that maybe my habit of asking questions was out of line here. I drank my beer and watched the singer. Hitler kept his back to her but I noticed she kept looking at him.

"What do you know about this Sagittarius?" I asked.

Hitler shrugged. "Very little."

Weill turned up again behind the bar and asked us if we wanted more beer. We said we didn't.

"Sagittarius?" Weill spoke up brightly. "Are you talking about that crank?"

"He's a crank, is he?" I said.

"That's not fair, Kurt," Hitler said. "He's a brilliant man, a biologist—"

"Who was thrown out of his job because he was insane!"

"That is unkind, Kurt," Hitler said reprovingly. "He was investigating the potential sentience of plant-life. A perfectly reasonable line of scientific enquiry."

From the corner of the room someone laughed jeeringly. It was a shaggy-haired old man sitting by himself with a glass of schnapps on the table in front of him.

Weill pointed at him. "Ask Albert. He knows about science."

Hitler pursed his lips and looked at the floor. "He's just an embittered old mathematics teacher—he's jealous of Felipe," he said quietly, so that the old man wouldn't hear.

"Who is he?" I asked Weill.

"Albert? A *really* brilliant man. He has never had the recognition he deserves. Do you want to meet him?"

But the shaggy man was leaving. He waved a hand at Hitler and Weill. "Kurt, Captain Hitler—good day."

"Good day, Doctor Einstein," muttered Hitler. He turned to me. "Where would you like to go now?"

"A tour of the places that sell jewellery, I guess," I said, fingering the pendant in my pocket. "I may be on the wrong track altogether, but it's the only track I can find at the moment."

We toured the jewellers. By nightfall we were nowhere nearer finding out who had owned the thing. I'd just have to get the truth out of Bismarck the next day, though I knew it wouldn't be easy. He wouldn't like answering my personal questions at all. Hitler dropped me off at the Precinct House where a cell had been converted into a bedroom for me.

I sat on the hard bed smoking and thinking. I was just about to get undressed and go to sleep when I started to think about the bar we'd been in earlier. I was sure someone there could help me. On impulse I left the cell and went out into the deserted street. It was still very hot and the sky was full of heavy clouds. Looked like a storm was due.

I got a cab back to the bar. It was still open.

Weill wasn't serving there now—he was playing the piano-accordion for the same girl singer I'd seen earlier. He nodded to me as I came in. I leant on the bar and ordered a beer from the barman.

When the number was over, Weill unstrapped his accordion and joined me. The girl followed him.

"Adolf not with you?" he said.

"He went home. He's a good friend of yours, is he?"

"Oh, we met years ago in Austria. He's a nice man, you know. He should never have become a policeman, he's too mild."

"That's the impression I got. Why did he ever join in the first place?"

Weill smiled and shook his head. He was a short, thin man, wearing heavy glasses. He had a large, sensitive mouth. "Sense of duty, perhaps. He has a great sense of duty. He is very religious, too—a devout Catholic. I think that weighs on him. You know these converts, they accept nothing, are torn by their consciences. I never yet met a happy Catholic convert."

"He seems to have a thing about Jews."

Weill frowned. "What sort of thing? I've never really noticed. Many of his friends are Jews. I am, and Sagittarius . . ."

"Sagittarius is a friend of his?"

"Oh, more an acquaintance I should think. I've seen them together a couple of times."

It began to thunder outside. Then it started to rain.

Weill walked towards the door and began to pull down the blind. Through the noise of the storm I heard another sound, a strange, metallic grinding sound, a crunching sound.

"What's that?" I called. Weill shook his head and walked back towards the bar. The place was empty now. "I'm going to have a look," I said.

I went to the door, opened it, and climbed the steps.

Marching across the ruins, illuminated by rapid flashes of lightning like gunfire, I saw a gigantic metal monster, as big as a tall building. Supported on four telescopic legs, it lumbered at right angles to the street. From its huge body and head the snouts of guns stuck out in all directions. Lightning sometimes struck it and it made an ear-shattering bell-like clang, paused to fire upwards at the source of the lightning, and march on.

I ran down the steps and flung open the door. Weill was tidying up the bar. I described what I'd seen.

"What is it, Weill?"

The short man shook his head. "I don't know. At a guess it is something Berlin's conquerors left behind."

"It looked as if it was made here . . ."

"Perhaps it was. After all, who conquered Berlin—?"

A woman screamed from a back room, high and brief.

Weill dropped a glass and ran towards the room. I followed.

He opened a door. The room was homely. A table covered by a thick, dark cloth, laid with salt and pepper, knives and forks, a piano near the window, a girl lying on the floor.

"Eva!" Weill gasped, kneeling beside the body.

I gave the room another once over. Standing on a small coffee table was a plant. It looked at first rather like a cactus of unpleasantly mottled green, though the top curved so that it resembled a snake about to strike. An eyeless, noseless snake—with a mouth. There was a mouth. It opened as I approached. There were teeth in the mouth—or rather thorns arranged the way teeth are. One thorn seemed to be missing near the front. I backed away from the plant and inspected the corpse. I found the thorn in her wrist. I left it there.

"She is dead," Weill said softly, standing up and looking around. "How?"

"She was bitten by that poisonous plant," I said.

"Plant . . . ? I must call the police."

"That wouldn't be wise at this stage maybe," I said as I left. I knew where I was going.

Bismarck's house—and the pleasure garden of Felipe Sagittarius.

It took me time to find a cab and I was soaked through when I did. I told the cabby to step on it.

I had the cab stop before we got to the house, paid it off and walked across the lawns. I didn't bother to ring the doorbell. I let myself in by the window, using my pocket glasscutter.

I heard voices coming from upstairs. I followed the sound until I located it—Bismarck's study. I inched the door open.

Hitler was there. He had a gun pointed at Otto von Bismarck who was still in full uniform. They both looked pale. Hitler's hand was shaking and Bismarck was moaning slightly.

Bismarck stopped moaning to say pleadingly, "I wasn't blackmailing Eva Braun, you fool—she liked me."

Hitler laughed curtly, half hysterically. "Like *you*—a fat old man."

"She liked fat old men."

"She wasn't that kind of girl."

"Who told you this, anyway?"

"The investigator told me some. And Weill rang me half an hour ago to tell me some more—also that Eva had been killed. I thought Sagittarius was my friend. I was wrong. He is your hired assassin. Well, tonight I intend to do my own killing."

"Captain Hitler—I am your superior officer!"

The gun wavered as Bismarck's voice recovered some of its authority. I realized that the Hi-Fi had been playing quietly all the time. Curiously it was Bartok's Fifth String Quartet.

Bismarck moved his hand. "You are completely mistaken. That man you hired to follow Eva here last night—he was Eva's ex-lover!"

Hitler's lip trembled.

"You knew," said Bismarck.

"I suspected it."

"You also knew the dangers of the garden, because Felipe had told you about them. The vines killed him as he sneaked toward the summer house."

The gun steadied. Bismarck looked scared.

He pointed at Hitler. "You killed him—not I!" he screamed. "You sent him to his death. You killed Stalin—out of jealousy. You hoped he would kill me and Eva first. You were too frightened, too weak, to confront any of us openly!"

Hitler shouted wordlessly, put both hands to the gun and pulled the trigger several times. Some of the shots went wide, but one hit Bismarck in his Iron Cross, pierced it and got him in the heart. He fell backwards and as he did so his uniform ripped apart and his helmet fell off. I ran into the room and took the gun from Hitler who was crying. I checked that Bismarck was dead. I saw what had caused the uniform to rip open. He had been wearing a corset—one of the bullets must have cut the cord. It was a heavy corset and had had a lot to hold in.

I felt sorry for Hitler. I helped him sit down as he sobbed. He looked small and wretched.

"What have I killed?" he stuttered. "What have I killed?"

"Did Bismarck send that plant to Eva Braun to silence her because I was getting too close?"

Hitler nodded, snorted and started to cry again.

I looked towards the door. A man stood there, hesitantly.

I put the gun on the mantelpiece.

It was Sagittarius.

He nodded to me.

"Hitler's just shot Bismarck," I explained.

"So it appears," he said.

"Bismarck had you send Eva Braun that plant, is that so?" I said.

"Yes. A beautiful cross between a common cactus, a Venus Flytrap and a rose—the venom was curare, of course."

Hitler got up and walked from the room. We watched him leave. He was still sniffling.

"Where are you going" I asked.

"To get some air," I heard him say as he went down the stairs.

"The repression of sexual desires," said Sagittarius seating himself in an armchair and resting his feet comfortably on Bismarck's corpse. "It is the cause of so much trouble. If only the passions that lie beneath the surface, the desires that are locked in the mind could be allowed to range free, what a better place the world would be."

"Maybe," I said.

"Are you going to make any arrests, Herr Aquilinas?"

"It's my job to make a report on my investigation, not to make arrests," I said.

"Will there be any repercussions concerned with this business?"

I laughed. "There are always repercussions," I told him.

From the garden came a peculiar barking noise.

"What's that?" I asked. "The wolfhounds?"

Sagittarius giggled. "No, no—the dog-plant, I fear."

I ran out of the room and down the stairs until I reached the kitchen. The sheet-covered corpse was still lying on the table. I was going to open the door on to the garden when I stopped and pressed my face to the window instead.

The whole garden was moving in what appeared to be an agitated dance. Foliage threshed about and, even with the door closed, the strange scent was even less bearable than it had been earlier.

I thought I saw a figure struggling with some thick-boled shrubs. I heard a growling noise, a tearing sound, a scream and a long drawn out groan.

Suddenly the garden was motionless.

I turned. Sagittarius stood behind me, his hands folded on his chest, his eyes staring down at the floor.

"It seems your dog-plant got him," I said.

"He knew me—he knew the garden."

"Suicide maybe?"

"Very likely." Sagittarius unfolded his hands and looked up at me. "I liked him, you know. He was something of a protégé. If you had not interfered none of this might have happened. He might have gone far with me to guide him."

"You'll find other protégés," I said.

"Let us hope so."

The sky outside began to lighten imperceptibly. The rain was now only a drizzle, falling on the thirsty leaves of the plants in the garden.

"Are you going to stay on here?" I asked him.

"Yes—I have the garden to work on. Bismarck's servants will look after me."

"I guess they will," I said.

I went back up the stairs and walked out of that house into the dawn, cold and rain-washed. I turned up my collar and began to climb across the ruins.

The Mountain

The last two men alive came out of the Lapp tent they had just raised for provisions.

"She's been here before us," said Nilsson. "It looks like she got the best of what there was."

Hallner shrugged. He had eaten so little for so long that food no longer held any great importance for him.

He looked about him. Lapp *kata* wigwams of wood and hides were spread around the immediate area of dry ground. Valuable skins had been left out to cure, reindeer horns to bleach, the doors unfastened so that anyone might enter the deserted homes.

Hallner rather regretted the passing of the Lapps. They had had no part in the catastrophe, no interest in wars or violence or competition. Yet they had been herded to the shelters with everyone else. And, like everyone else, they had perished either by direct bombing, radiation poisoning or asphyxiation.

He and Nilsson had been in a forgotten meteorological station close to the Norwegian border. When they finally repaired their radio, the worst was over. Fall-out had by this time finished off the tribesmen in Indonesian jungles, the workers in remote districts of China, the hill-billies in the Rockies, the crofters in Scotland. Only freak weather conditions, which had been part of their reason for visiting the station earlier in the year, had so far prevented the lethal rain from falling in this area of Swedish Lappland.

They had known themselves, perhaps instinctively, to be the last two human-beings alive, until Nilsson found the girl's tracks coming from the south and heading north. Who she was, how she'd escaped, they couldn't guess, but they had changed their direction from north-east to north and began to follow. Two days later they had found the Lapp camp.

Now they stared ahead of them at the range of ancient mountains. It was three a.m., but the sun still hung a bloody spread on the horizon for it was summer—the six-week summer of the Arctic when the sun never fully set, when the snows of the mountains melted and ran down to form the rivers, lakes and marshes of the lowlands where only the occasional Lapp camp, or the muddy scar of a broad reindeer path, told of the presence of the few men who lived here during the winter months.

Suddenly, as he looked away from the range, the camp aroused some emotion akin to pity in Hallner's mind. He remembered the despair of the dying man who had told them, on his radio, what had happened to the world.

Nilsson had entered another hut and came out shaking a packet of raisins. "Just what we need," he said.

"Good," said Hallner, and he sighed inaudibly. The clean, orderly nature of the little primitive village was spoiled for him by the sight he had witnessed earlier at the stream which ran through the camp. There had been simple drinking cups of clay or bone side by side with an aluminum dish and an empty Chase and Sanborne coffee jar, a cheap plastic plate and a broken toy car.

"Shall we go?" Nilsson said, and began to make his way out of the camp.

Not without certain trepidation, Hallner followed behind his friend who marched towards the mountains without looking back or even from side to side.

Nilsson had a goal and, rather than sit down, brood and die when the inescapable finally happened, Hallner was prepared to go along with him on this quest for the girl.

And, he admitted, there was a faint chance that if the winds continued to favour them, they might have a chance of life. In which case there was a logical reason for Nilsson's obsessional tracking of the woman.

His friend was impatient of his wish to walk slowly and savour the atmosphere of the country which seemed so detached and removed, uninvolved with him, disdainful. That there were things which had no emotional relationship with him, had given him a slight surprise at first, and even now he walked the marshy ground with a feeling of abusing privacy, of destroying the sanctity of a place where there was so little hint of humanity; where men had been rare and had not been numerous or frequent enough visitors to have left the aura of their passing behind them.

So it was with a certain shock that he later observed the print of small rubber soles on the flat mud near a river.

"She's still ahead of us," said Nilsson, pleased at this sign, "and not so very far ahead. Little more than a day. We're catching up."

Suddenly, he realized that he was displeased by the presence of the bootprints, almost resentful of Nilsson's recognition of their being there when, alone, he might have ignored them. He reflected that Nilsson's complete acceptance of the sex of the boots' wearer was entirely founded on his own wishes.

The river poured down towards the flat lake on their left, clear, bright melted snow from the mountains. Brown, sun-dried rocks stood out of it, irregularly spaced, irregularly contoured, affording them a means of crossing the swift waters.

There were many such rivers, running down the slopes of the foothills like silver veins to fill the lakes and spread them further over the marshland. There were hills on the plateau where trees crowded together, fir and silver birch, like survivors of a flood jostling for a place on the high ground. There were ridges which sometimes hid sight of the tall mountains in front of them, green with grass and reeds, studded with gorse.

He had never been so far into mountain country before and this range was one of the oldest in the world; there were no sharp peaks as in the Alps. These were worn and solid and they had lived through eons of change and metamorphosis to have earned their right to solitude, to permanency.

Snow still spattered their sides like galaxies against the grey-green moss and rock. Snow-fields softened their lines.

Nilsson was already crossing the river, jumping nimbly from rock to rock, his film-star's profile sometimes silhouetted against the clear, sharp sky, the pack on his back like Christian's load in the *Pilgrim's Progress*. Hallner smiled to himself. Only indirectly was Nilsson heading for salvation.

Now he followed.

He balanced himself in his flat, leather-soled boots and

sprang from the first rock to the second, righted his balance again and sprang to the next. The river boiled around the rocks, rushing towards the lake, to lose itself in the larger waters. He jumped again, slipped and was up to his knees in the ice-cold torrent. He raised his small knapsack over his head and, careless now, did not bother to clamber back to the rocks, but pushed on, waist-deep, through the freezing river. He came gasping to the bank and was helped to dry land by Nilsson who shook his head and laughed.

"You're hopeless!"

"It's all right," he said, "the sun will dry me out soon."

But both had walked a considerable distance and both were tiring. The sun had now risen, round and hazy red in the pale, cold sky, but it was still difficult to gauge the passage of the hours. This, also, added to the detached air of timelessness which the mountain and the plateaux possessed. There was no night—only a slight alteration in the quality of the day. And although the heat was ninety degrees fahrenheit, the sky still looked cold, for it took more than the brief six weeks of summer to change the character of this wintry Jotunheim.

He thought of Jotunheim, the Land of Giants, and understood better the myths of his ancestors with their accent on man's impermanency—the mortality of their very gods, their bleak worship of the forces of nature. Only here could he appreciate that the life span of the world itself might be infinite, but the life span of its denizens was necessarily subject to inevitable metamorphosis and eventual death. And, as he thought, his impression of the country changed so that instead of the feeling of invading sanctified ground, he felt as if a privilege had been granted him and he had been allowed, for a few moments of his short life, to experience eternity.

The mountains themselves might crumble in time, the planet cease to exist, but that it would be reincarnated he was certain. And this gave him humility and hope for his own life and, for the first time, he began to think that he might have a purpose in continuing to live, after all.

He did not dwell on the idea, since there was no need to.

They came with relief to a dry place where they lighted a fire and cooked the last of their bacon in their strong metal frying pan. They ate their food and cleaned the pan with ashes from the fire, and he took it down to the nearest river

and rinsed it, stooping to drink a little, not too much, since
he had learned from his mistake earlier, for the water could
be like a drug so that one craved to drink more and more until exhausted.

He realized, vaguely, that they had to keep as fit as possible. For one of them to come to harm could mean danger
for them both. But the thought meant little. There was no
sense of danger here.

He slept and, before he fell into a deep, dreamless sleep,
he had a peculiar impression of being at once vast and tiny.
His eyes closed, his body relaxed, he felt so big that the
atoms of his body, in relation to the universe, hardly had existence, that the universe had become an unobservable electron, present but unseen. And yet, intratemporally, he had the
impression that he was as small as an electron so that he
existed in a gulf, a vacuum containing no matter whatso-
ever.

A mystic, perhaps, would have taken this for some holy experience, but he could do no more than accept it, feeling no
need to interpret it. Then he slept.

Next morning, Nilsson showed him a map he had found in
the village.

"That's where she's going," he said, pointing at a mountain
in the distance. "It's the highest in this section and the second
highest in the entire range. Wonder why she'd want to climb
a mountain?"

Hallner shook his head.

Nilsson frowned. "You're in a funny mood. Think you
won't have a chance with the girl?" When Hallner didn't answer, Nilsson said impatiently. "Maybe she's got some idea
that she's safer on top of a mountain. With luck, we'll find
out soon. Ready to go?"

Hallner nodded.

They moved on in silence.

The range was discernibly closer, now, and Hallner could
look at individual mountains. Although looming over the others, the one they headed for looked squat, solid, somehow
older than the rest, even.

For a while they were forced to concentrate on the ground
immediately in front of them, for it had become little more
than thick mud which oozed over their boots and threatened

to pull them down, to join, perhaps, the remains of prehistoric saurians which lay many feet below.

Nilsson said little and Hallner was glad that no demands were made on him.

It was as if the edge of the world lay beyond the last ragged pile of mountains, or as if they had left Earth and were in a concave saucer surrounded by mountains, containing only the trees and the lakes, marshes and hills.

He had the feeling that this place was so inviolable, so invulnerable, miles from the habitation of men so that for the first time he fully realized that men had ceased to exist along with their artifacts. It was as if they had never really existed at all or that their spell of dominance had appeared and disappeared in practically the same moment of time.

But now, for the first time since he had heard the hysterical voice on the radio, he felt some stirring of his old feeling return as he stared at the great mountain, heavy and huge against the ice-blue sky. But it was transformed. Ambition had become the summit, reward the silence, the peace that waited at the peak. Curiosity was the desire to discover the cause of a freakish colouring half-way up the mountain and fear did not exist for in these enigmatic mountains there was no uncertainty. A vast, well-less womb with the infinite sky curving above and the richly-coloured scenery, blues, whites, browns and greens, surrounding them, complete, cutting them off from even the sight of the ruined outside world.

It was a snow-splashed paradise, where well-fed wolves left the carcasses of their prey to lap at the pure water of the rivers. A wilderness replete with life, with lemming, reindeer, wolverine, wolf and even bear, with lakes swarming with freshwater herring and the air a silent gulf above them to set off the smack of a hawk's wing. Night could not fall and so the potenital dangers of savage wildlife, which could not be felt in the vastness of a world where there was room for everything, could never be realized.

Occasionally, they would discover a slain reindeer, bones dull and white, its hide tattered and perishing, and they would feel no horror, no emotion at all, for although its obvious killer, the wolverine, was a cruel beast, destroying often for the sake of destroying, the wolverine was not aware of its crime and therefore it was no crime at all.

Everything here was self-sufficient, moulded by fate, by circumstance, but since it did not analyse, since it accepted itself and its conditions without question, it was therefore more complete than the men who walked and stumbled across its uncompromising terrain.

At length they came to the sloping, grass-covered roots of the mountain and he trembled with emotion to see it rising so high above him, the grass fading, parting to reveal the tumbled rock and the rock vanishing higher up beneath banks of snow.

"She will have taken the easiest face," Nilsson decided, looking at the map he had found in the camp. "It will mean crossing two snow-fields."

They rested on the last of the grass. And he looked down over the country through which they had passed, unable to talk or describe his feelings. It possessed no horizon, for mountains were on all sides, and within the mountains he saw rivers and lakes, tree-covered hills, all of which had taken on fresh, brighter colourings, the lakes reflecting the red of the sun and the blue of the sky and giving them subtly different qualities.

He was glad they were taking the easiest face for he felt no need, here, to rest or to temper himself.

For a while he felt complete with the country, ready to climb upwards because he would rather do so and because the view from the peak would also be different, add, perhaps, to the fullness of his experience.

He realized, as they got up, that this was not what Nilsson was feeling. Hallner had almost forgotten about the girl.

They began to climb. It was tiring, but not difficult for initially the slope was gradual, less than forty-five degrees. They came to the first snow-field which was slightly below them, climbed downwards carefully, but with relief.

Nilsson had taken a stick from the Lapp camp. He took a step forward, pressing the stick into the snow ahead of him, took another step, pressed the stick down again.

Hallner followed, treading cautiously in his friend's footsteps, little pieces of frozen snow falling into his boots. He knew that Nilsson was trying to judge the snow-field's thickness. Below it a deep river coursed and he thought he heard its musical rushing beneath his feet. He noted, also, that his feet now felt frozen and uncomfortable.

Very slowly they crossed the snow-field and at length, after a long time, they were safely across and sat down to rest for a while, preparing for the steeper climb ahead.

Nilsson eased his pack off his shoulders and leaned against it, staring back at the field.

"No tracks," he mused. "Perhaps she crossed further down."

"Perhaps she didn't come here after all." Hallner spoke with effort. He was not really interested.

"Don't be a fool." Nilsson rose and hefted his pack on to his back again.

They climbed over the sharp rocks separating the two snow-fields and once again underwent the danger of crossing the second field.

Hallner sat down to rest again, but Nilsson climbed on. After a few moments, Hallner followed and saw that Nilsson had stopped and was frowning at the folded map in his hand.

When he reached Nilsson he saw that the mountain now curved upwards around a deep, wide indentation. Across this, a similar curve went up towards the summit. It looked a decidedly easier climb than the one which faced them.

Nilsson swore.

"The damned map's misled us—or else the position of the fields has altered. We've climbed the wrong face."

"Should we go back down again?" Hallner asked uninterestedly.

"No—there's not much difference—we'd have still lost a lot of time."

Where the two curves joined, there was a ridge high above them which would take them across to the face which they should have climbed. This was getting close to the peak, so that in fact, there would be no advantage even when they reached the other side.

"No wonder we missed her tracks," Nilsson said pettishly. "She'll be at the summit by now."

"How do you know she climbed this mountain?" Hallner wondered why he had not considered this earlier.

Nilsson waved the map. "You don't think Lapps need these? No—*she* left it behind."

"Oh . . ." Hallner stared down at the raw, tumbling rocks which formed an almost sheer drop beneath his feet.

"No more resting," Nilsson said. "We've got a lot of time to make up."

He followed behind Nilsson who foolishly expended his energy in swift, savage ascents and was showing obvious signs of exhaustion before they ever reached the ridge.

Unperturbed by the changed situation, Hallner climbed after him, slowly and steadily. The ascent was taking longer, was more difficult and he, also, was tired, but he possessed no sense of despair.

Panting, Nilsson waited for him on a rock close to the ridge, which formed a narrow strip of jumbled rocks slanting upwards towards the peak. On one side of it was an almost sheer drop going down more than a hundred feet, and on the other the rocky sides sloped steeply down to be submerged in a dazzling expanse of faintly creaking ice—a glacier.

"I'm going to have to leave you behind if you don't move faster," Nilsson panted.

Hallner put his head slightly on one side and peered up the mountain. Silently, he pointed.

"God! Everything's against us, today," Nilsson kicked at a loose piece of rock and sent it out into space. It curved and plummeted down, but they could not see or hear it fall.

The mist, which Hallner had noted, came rolling swiftly towards them, obscuring the other peaks, boiling in across the range.

"Will it affect us?" Hallner asked.

"It's sure to!"

"How long will it stay?"

"A few minutes or several hours, it's impossible to tell. If we stay where we are we could very well freeze to death. If we go on there's a chance of reaching the summit and getting above it. Willing to risk it?"

This last remark was a sneering challenge.

"Why yes, of course," Hallner said.

Now that the fact had been mentioned, he noted for the first time that he was cold. But the coldness was not uncomfortable.

They had no ropes, no climbing equipment of any kind, and even his boots were flat-soled city boots. As the mist poured in, its grey, shifting mass limiting vision almost utterly at times, they climbed on, keeping together by shouts.

Once, he could hardly see at all, reached a rock, felt about it with his boot, put his weight on the rock, slipped, clung to the rock and felt both feet go sliding free in space just as the mist parted momentarily to show him the creaking glacier far below him. And something else—a black, spread-out shadow blemishing the pure expanse of ice.

He scrabbled at the rock with his toes, trying to swing himself back to the main part of the ridge, got an insecure toehold and clung himself sideways to the comparative safety of the narrow causeway. He breathed quickly and shallowly and shook with reaction. Then he arose and continued on up the slanting ridge.

A while later, when the main thickness of the mist had rolled past and now lay above the glacier, he saw that they had crossed the ridge and were on the other side without his having realized it.

He could now see Nilsson climbing with obvious difficulty towards what he had called the 'false summit'. The real summit could not be seen, was hidden by the other, but there was now only another hundred feet to climb.

They rested on the false summit, unable to see much that was below them for, although the mist was thinner, it was thick enough to hide most of the surrounding mountains. Sometimes it would part so that they could see fragments of mountains, patches of distant lakes, but little else.

Hallner looked at Nilsson. The other man's handsome face had taken on a set, obstinate look. One hand was bleeding badly.

"Are you all right?" Hallner nodded his head towards the bleeding hand.

"Yes!"

Hallner lost interest since it was evident he could not help Nilsson in his present mood.

He noted that the mist had penetrated his thin jacket and his whole body was damp and chilled. His own hands were torn and grazed and his body was bruised, aching, but he was still not discomfited. He allowed Nilsson to start off first and then forced himself on the last stage of the climb.

By the time he reached the snowless summit, the air was bright, the mist had disappeared and the sun shone in the clear sky.

He flung himself down close to Nilsson who was again peering at his map.

He lay panting, sprawled awkwardly on the rock and stared out over the world.

There was nothing to say. The scene itself, although magnificent, was not what stopped him from talking, stopped his mind from reasoning, as if time had come to a standstill, as if the passage of the planet through space had been halted. He existed, like a monument, petrified, unreasoning, absorbing. He drank in eternity.

Why hadn't the dead human race realized this? It was only necessary to exist, not to be trying constantly to prove you existed when the fact was plain.

Plain to him, he realized, because he had climbed a mountain. This knowledge was his reward. He had not received any ability to think with greater clarity, or a vision to reveal the secret of the universe, or an experience of ecstasy. He had been given, by himself, by his own action, insensate peace, the infinite tranquillity of *existing*.

Nilsson's harsh, disappointed tones invaded this peace.

"I could have sworn she would climb up here. Maybe she did. Maybe we were too late and she's gone back down again?"

Hallner remembered the mark he had seen on the glacier. Now he knew what it had been.

"I saw something back on the ridge," he said. "On the glacier. A human figure, I think."

"What? Why didn't you tell me?"

"I don't know."

"Was she alive? Think of the importance of this—if she is alive we can start the human race all over again. What's the matter with you, Hallner? Have you gone crazy with shock or something? *Was she alive?*"

"Perhaps—I don't know."

"You don't—" Nilsson snarled in disbelief and began scrabbling back the way he had come.

"You heartless bastard! Supposing she's hurt—injured!"

Hallner watched Nilsson go cursing and stumbling, sometimes falling, on his over-rapid descent of the mountain. He saw him rip off his pack and fling it aside, nearly staggering over the ridge as he began to climb down it.

Hallner thought dispassionately that Nilsson would kill himself if he continued so heedlessly.

Then he returned his gaze to the distant lakes and trees below him.

He lay on the peak of the mountain, sharing its existence. He was immobile, he did not even blink as he took in the view. It seemed that he was part of the rock, part of the mountain itself.

A little later there came an aching yell which died away into the silence. But Hallner did not hear it.

DAWsf
BOOKS

Presenting MICHAEL MOORCOCK
in DAW editions

The Elric Novels

☐ **ELRIC OF MELNIBONE** (#UW1356—$1.50)
☐ **THE SAILOR ON THE SEAS OF FATE** (#UW1434—$1.50)
☐ **THE WEIRD OF THE WHITE WOLF** (#UW1390—$1.50)
☐ **THE VANISHING TOWER** (#UW1406—$1.50)
☐ **THE BANE OF THE BLACK SWORD** (#UW1421—$1.50)
☐ **STORMBRINGER** (#UW1335—$1.50)

The Runestaff Novels

☐ **THE JEWEL IN THE SKULL** (#UW1419—$1.50)
☐ **THE MAD GOD'S AMULET** (#UW1391—$1.50)
☐ **THE SWORD OF THE DAWN** (#UW1392—$1.50)
☐ **THE RUNESTAFF** (#UW1422—$1.50)

The Oswald Bastable Novels

☐ **THE WARLORD OF THE AIR** (#UW1380—$1.50)
☐ **THE LAND LEVIATHAN** (#UW1448—$1.50)

The Michael Kane Novels

☐ **CITY OF THE BEAST** (#UW1436—$1.50)
☐ **LORD OF THE SPIDERS** (#UW1443—$1.50)
☐ **MASTERS OF THE PIT** (#UW1450—$1.50)

Other Titles

☐ **LEGENDS FROM THE END OF TIME** (#UY1281—$1.25)
☐ **A MESSIAH AT THE END OF TIME** (#UW1358—$1.50)
☐ **DYING FOR TOMORROW** (#UW1366—$1.50)
☐ **THE RITUALS OF INFINITY** (#UW1404—$1.50)

If you wish to order these titles,

please see the coupon in

the back of this book.

Recommended for Star Warriors!

The Dorsai Novels of Gordon R. Dickson

☐ DORSAI! (#UE1342—$1.75)
☐ SOLDIER, ASK NOT (#UE1339—$1.75)
☐ TACTICS OF MISTAKE (#UW1279—$1.50)
☐ NECROMANCER (#UE1353—$1.75)

The Commodore Grimes Novels of
A. Bertram Chandler

☐ THE BIG BLACK MARK (#UW1335—$1.50)
☐ THE WAY BACK (#UW1352—$1.50)
☐ STAR COURIER (#UY1292—$1.25)
☐ TO KEEP THE SHIP (#UE1385—$1.75)
☐ THE FAR TRAVELER (#UW1444—$1.50)

The Dumarest of Terra Novels of E. C. Tubb

☐ JACK OF SWORDS (#UY1239—$1.25)
☐ SPECTRUM OF A FORGOTTEN SUN (#UY1265—$1.25)
☐ HAVEN OF DARKNESS (#UY1299—$1.25)
☐ PRISON OF NIGHT (#UW1346—$1.50)
☐ INCIDENT ON ATH (#UW1389—$1.50)
☐ THE QUILLIAN SECTOR (#UW1426—$1.50)

The Daedalus Novels of Brian M. Stableford

☐ THE FLORIANS (#UY1255—$1.25)
☐ CRITICAL THRESHOLD (#UY1282—$1.25)
☐ WILDEBLOOD'S EMPIRE (#UW1331—$1.50)
☐ THE CITY OF THE SUN (#UW1377—$1.50)
☐ BALANCE OF POWER (#UE1437—$1.75)

If you wish to order these titles,

please use the coupon in

the back of this book.

DAW presents TANITH LEE

"A brilliant supernova in the firmament of SF"—Progressef

☐ **THE BIRTHGRAVE.** "A big, rich, bloody swords-and-sorcery epic with a truly memorable heroine—as tough as Conan the Barbarian but more convincing."—*Publishers Weekly.* (#UW1177—$1.50)

☐ **VAZKOR, SON OF VAZKOR.** The world-shaking saga that is the sequel to THE BIRTHGRAVE . . . a hero with super-powers seeks vengeance on his witch mother. (#UJ1350—$1.95)

☐ **QUEST FOR THE WHITE WITCH.** The mighty conclusion of Vazkor's quest is a great novel of sword & sorcery. (#UJ1357—$1.95)

☐ **DEATH'S MASTER.** "Compelling and evocative . . . possesses a sexual explicitness and power only intimated in myth and fairy tales."—*Publishers Weekly.* (#UJ1441—$1.95)

☐ **NIGHT'S MASTER.** "Erotic without being graphic . . . a satisfying fantasy . . . It could easily become a cult item. Recommended."—*Library Journal.* (#UE1414—$1.75)

☐ **DON'T BITE THE SUN.** "Probably the finest book you have ever published."—Marion Zimmer Bradley. (#UE1486—$1.75)

☐ **DRINKING SAPPHIRE WINE.** How the hero/heroine of Four BEE city finally managed to outrage the system! (#UY1277—$1.25)

☐ **THE STORM LORD.** A Panoramic novel of swordplay and of a man seeking his true inheritance on an alien world. (#UJ1361—$1.95)

DAW BOOKS are represented by the publishers of Signet and Mentor Books, THE NEW AMERICAN LIBRARY, INC.
